Master of the Eclipse

Master
of the Eclipse

and Other Stories

Etel Adnan

Interlink Books

An imprint of Interlink Publishing Group, Inc.
Northampton, Massachusetts

This edition first published in 2023 by

INTERLINK BOOKS
An imprint of Interlink Publishing Group, Inc.
46 Crosby Street
Northampton, Massachusetts 01060
www.interlinkbooks.com

Library of Congress Cataloging-in-Publication Data:
Adnan, Etel.
The master of the eclipse / by Etel Adnan. — 1st American ed.
p. cm.
Short stories.
ISBN 978-1-62371-711-7 (pbk.)
I. Title.
PS3551.D65M37 2009
813'.54—dc22
2008052435

Printed and bound in the United States of America

to Hans-Ulrich Müller-Schwefe

Part One

Master of the Eclipse

> … *what are poets for in these destitute times?*
> —Hölderlin, *Elegies*

> … *but only poets found that which will endure*
> —Hölderlin, *Hymns*

S itting in this bus I am, as in any vehicle, be it plane, train, truck, or boat, myself an object in a magic container whose inner sides are at this moment in a state of suspension. Memories are projected on them like shadows running back and forth in a space both existing and unreal. What have I left behind? What kind of messages are trying to reach me as I ride from one point in the north of Sicily to the other?

We are in the summer of '91. Bombs are falling mercilessly on Iraq; the country is being destroyed; from the start the process looked irreversible and the outcome bound to be annihilation.

There's only one other person on the bus. We boarded it together but the man in the seat in front of me looked distant this morning; he barely said hello and now he is sleeping, or pretending to be asleep.

I would probably need a foreword to my story: in Europe there's a proliferation of festivals. It is exhilarating to be offered such a quantity of programs, to know that the masters are being played more than ever, that operas are sung nightly in the beautiful concert halls of the Western world. Then another feeling creeps in, of uneasiness, confusion, and helplessness. Are these countries considering "culture" a remedy? Do they believe it is redeeming? But then, do we have to always think in terms of punishment and redemption?

Three or four days have passed since I came to Gibelina, invited to its summer festival. I arrived at night and was led to a room barely furnished, smelling of recently washed sheets, with a window covered with white embroidered curtains. That's indeed a Mediterranean little hotel, I thought with pleasure, everything will be charming now that things already have begun to look familiar.

In the morning I had breakfast with a good appetite, congratulating myself for being in a corner of Italy I had not yet visited. This is not Tuscany, I thought, when I noticed the flamboyant light entering the door; this is almost my part of the world, this Mediterranean with its perpetually youngish sun and the sense of well-being it provides.

I wondered if any of the other customers were also guests of the festival. I asked and was told that the musicians who played the night before had already left for Palermo and that some Arab poets were scheduled to arrive in the afternoon or a bit later.

While drinking coffee I am in the midst of the Gulf War: a movie is passing in front of my eyes but the images are not in black and white, they are the color of my skin. They tell me that Iraq is being crushed under bombs and warn me to be careful, not to show too much emotion, to keep my worries under a lid when they are of no interest to most people. This recurring need for dissimulation creates a kind of a shield, a second self so to speak, that censors thoughts, or sometimes erases them altogether. In Gibelina I have to be an innocent visitor who came to read some poetry.

There are buckets planted with flowers and the heat is rising. The air is dry, austere, as in the days of imperial Rome, the way I like it. Francesca has arrived and is running to greet me. She is an angel escaped from a Fra Angelico painting, bringing the kinder side of the world.

She leads me to an immense stone-built hall, recently inaugurated, she says, whose space has been turned into some primitive cave where my eyes decipher the paintings of a contemporary artist, who, like the ancient ones from Italy, did not sign his name under what he had carefully designed. These are Pizzi Cannella's *Diary of a War*, Francesca tells me with pride.

Canvases, earth-colored, brutally large and brutally spare, cover the walls of this municipal museum. Lines of black paint run over them but define almost nothing. The canvases are either left bare or are covered with layers of diluted ochre acrylics. On the largest surfaces other lines, white sepulchral threads, delineate softly, sinuously, what appear to be shapes of continents deformed by invisible pressures. Dispersed marks seem to signify airports or military outposts. They could also mean tracks left by the American armored vehicles that are equipped with low-level radioactive weapons. The whole installation is about deliquescence. It tells that the country is being disintegrated before our eyes. Iraq—with its battlegrounds—is being transferred here, from thousands of miles away, by an Italian painter who's declaring his horror through maps seemingly made of mud, asphalt, and pulverized bones. Little by little one sees that he has established for his viewers the geometry of his own soul along the frontiers of a distant and sacrificial land.

We returned to the hotel for lunch. We were at the beginning of the meal when a round figure, with his back turned to the light, entered the dining room. I noticed his crumpled clothes, saw him sit by the wall, on my left, then paid no more attention to him. Suddenly, he stood up, stared fixedly at us, and recognizing him, I shouted his name: Buland!

Francesca asked him to join our table. He was one of the poets invited for the reading that was going to take place that evening. I was shocked to reencounter the young poet who had danced a whole night in Baghdad some fifteen years back in time.

He looked a man exhausted. Francesca said that she wasn't surprised that we knew each other. He didn't comment. She tried to create a conversation. She reminded us that we were both to participate in the reading, which had been announced all over town and on the radio. She added that it had already stirred a great deal of excitement. It was too hot, but we nonetheless drank some wine, and Buland kept drinking.

༺༻

The place was overflowing with people: they had come from Gibelina but also from neighboring villages. The Center was buzzing with expectation. The mayor delivered a speech, and then a Tunisian poet was the first to face the audience.

The readings were staged with the solemnity of a mass in a basilica: two lecterns stood side by side, one for the Arab poet, one for his translator. The Arab poet had to go first and an actress had been brought from Naples for the Italian version. In fact, her long hair was "catching fire," reflecting the light of the long candles that were the guardian angels of the ceremony. Then the chandeliers, which in daytime offered such a contrast with the austere stone walls, were dimmed.

The Tunisian poet was obviously impressed. His monotonous voice delivered a litany of poetic themes: the ever-present sea, fishermen from Sfax, the desert, again and always, and pre-Islamic Laila whose rivers of tears her lover maddeningly navigated. He overran his time. The Neapolitan beauty showed her discomfort in the heat and her impatience. When her turn came, I have to say, she brought life to the poems.

Buland came to the fore. He stood there, holding a few sheets of paper… he sized up the room and the people who were holding their breath in the semi-darkness. He knew he was the center of the whole event. He was here for his own sake and for Iraq's. Gathered in himself were all the reasons these people were worried and had come to show solidarity. He was a messenger. The gods of his country had sent him. He wouldn't let them down.

The audience was already won. He could have read anything, recited the whole of the Arabic alphabet, given the complete list of Iraqi cities, he could have repeated in their usual order the ninety-nine names of God, it would have been poetry and they would have applauded.

He was standing, slightly trembling because of the heat, because of his emotions, knowing that while he was getting the audience's attention, houses in Iraq were crumbling… the dust they were making over there was rising like a curtain between him and the audience.

He spoke to them through his poem of Zenobia, queen of Palmyra, who came close to defeating Rome with her army of slow camel drivers, Bedu fighters, fierce caravan chiefs and barefooted servants… They applauded as if, though Italians, they wished the Arab queen had won. Then a poem was heard of wounds bleeding on maps, of olive trees chopped and exported in crates, of mirrors in front of which soldiers combed their hair. He looked through a distant window, didn't see the moon, but evoked her. Then he sounded meditative, confiding that he felt most alive when dead. He added that angels came regularly to switch on fluorescent lights over prison courtyards in order to record the secret patterns that insects make when they dance at night in their midst. He was becoming more and more a man who had returned from outer space and who was trying to secure the ground under his feet to reorient himself. He felt truly loved.

He picked up a new bunch of papers. Taking his time, he read slowly, barely audible. Gradually his voice picked up momentum and he spoke of women, he explained in verse after verse that they were treacherous, but justified to be so, because divine love was treacherous too. He said that sleeping with a woman was like coming down the Tigris on a narrow craft all by oneself. He did his best not to cry.

I keep hearing him say that he feared life more than death, then reciting as if it were a dirge a poem about bulls tumbling in fog and death sentences pursuing the East… once it was about stallions and dripping faucets, then about sounds of stampedes and of blowing trumpets… "I was swimming in the turbulent waters of my soul," I remember him stating clearly; then he made us understand how rage is a form of meditation. Mixing talk with his poems, he was going back and forth, declaring that emigrants suffer from knots, ulcers, cancer, that their mind is chillier than ice, and, when someone interrupted, to shout that some immigrants are often ecstatic about the simple though miraculous fact of having at last a job, he went on reading about people drinking seawater and women wading in the twin rivers of Iraq; of wolves wearing sheepskins and of deer leaving the forest and dying on kitchen floors. He explained that words send back to you your own image, that they blind you by deflecting to your brain the sunrays of an August day.

Now, some fifteen years later, I am again hearing bombs falling on Baghdad. They are shattering my windows all the way here in California. Thousands of dead already and the war is at its beginning, and the National Library, with its medieval manuscripts, has been set on fire and a big chunk of humanity's memory has been destroyed; all this before large-scale killing has even started. Who is trying to eradicate the past and the present of the Arabs?

He stopped. The actress didn't need to take her turn. The public had understood; it was enchanted, and applauded for a long time. At the end he was exhausted and all he could think about was that he had well earned his ticket.

⌣⟜⟊⟊

A reception was held late that night. People gathered around him, wanting his opinion on Iraq's invasion of Kuwait but he kept repeating that he had none. A couple of hours later when two musicians, an Egyptian oud player and an Iraqi singer, showed up, Buland abruptly left the room. The rest of us stayed. The music was filled with longing; it seemed that the ancient melodies were sorrowfully commenting on the perennial presence of war.

The next day as we were free of obligations Francesca offered to take us on a visit to old Gibelina.

She led us to the top of a hill where old Gibelina used to stand before an earthquake had devastated it completely. The whole scene was eerie. They had bulldozed the remnants of the town, mixing dead bodies with broken walls, twisted pipes, furniture, toys… the gigantic open wound that the town had become had then been covered with a thick layer of white chalk. Then an artist had painted on the white slopes large grids of black paint and other designs that created a funereal, sacred desolation, as if in commemoration of some ancient god's power. Indeed, sometimes a landscape takes the form of our soul, and that was the case. This place was saying that men are not the sole actors in the universe but that, obviously, unknown powers interact with us outside our wills. We give them the generic name of Death. But there was no death on that hill, rather the telling of an ongoing tragedy, for which this site, like Baghdad over there, was providing the stage.

Throughout the visit it was hard to admit that the poet walking next to me had ever been the dazzling young man that I had met in Baghdad. He was now a bull: stocky, diffident, speaking silent rage and pain. While we were chatting he was, underneath his muted ways, bleeding. The destroyed grounds we were walking on, the festival itself and the poems that he had recited the night before as a series of funeral orations, indeed perpetuated the proclaimed sacredness of the site. They were also, strangely, the mirror image of what was going on in his own country.

Drastic sanctions were suffocating Iraq while bombings were going on. The Gulf War was the first round of the destruction of Iraq, one of the bloodiest bullfights in history: the horse-riding (or airplane-piloting) picadors had carefully weakened the bull with their lances for twelve long years so that the matador could come in for the final kill.

What is man other than pounds of water mixed with flesh and bones, articulated in such ways that he can stand wobbling on two legs and sometimes look at stars, and sometimes fertilize a female, and produce invisible waves that we name thoughts, and often tears that never relieve the pain. What is he if not a mass of confusion always searching for the very thing that he will refuse to grasp whenever the grasping becomes possible? Who is this being wearing bullet-proof jackets, who has to think that he's courageous and right and has to steal from the poor in order to feed the rich? And the poet ends up surrounded by sharks who chase him down into the deep.

❧

The man whose ghost is visiting me tonight in my California room has died in London. He had run away from the institution where his only son had committed him for alcoholism and demented behavior. He had joined the world of the homeless and been found under a bench near Paddington Station. The police said that he had been vomiting blood. Through some papers stuffed in his pocket they traced him back to his latest residence. His son had an obituary published in some newspapers so that the Arabs would know that one of their famous poets had died. The date of his birth was not mentioned, only the day of his passing.

Now the ghost is reciting litanies of saints, the long list of the friends of the deceased, who through the years had run like rats from basement to cave, from prison cells to torture chambers, discoursing on the blank faces of the hangmen and the differing voices of the dying. The ghost is telling me that the best burial we can perform for a friend is to tell the story:

In the middle of the seventies, I went to Baghdad to participate in a gathering of painters and poets. The visit introduced me to a space where the Tigris predominated; rose-colored mud streaming alongside the waters were mixed with fragments of sky. I spent my days contemplating that phenomenon while nights were filled with festivities. The continuum of pure time had embarked us along its flow.

Spring easily becomes mythical in Iraq. The breeze pulls out of the subsoil the first flowers of the ever-present desert, gods spring out too. There were many parties all around town. Small groups met in modest houses harboring musicians, poets, painters, all living legends. One evening when I went to hear a famous oud player, a dozen or so young men were already there and it turned out that they were all poets. Animated conversations were rising above the heavy clouds of tobacco smoke. Through that bluish fog I heard poetry recited, one voice after another, until the youngest rose, and a train of words went through the room and over the land and on the uncharted surfaces of our souls. Those poems put us all, it seemed, in a trance, because after a while the whole room stood and the men started to dance in circles. They danced, and at the end the oud player joined us, and we were all turning without a break, without a sound.

The next day there was one more reception, this time a dinner for some two hundred people. The young man sitting next to me on my right was none other than the flamboyant young poet that I had heard sing the night before. He asked me if I felt well received in Baghdad. Without waiting for my answer he introduced himself as a student of history and added in the same breath that he was primarily a poet and that poetry was all that mattered to him. I was amazed by his extreme beauty and he felt it and smiled most disarmingly when serving some dessert on my plate. With a kind of childish happiness he declared that he knew some of my poems by heart, and followed by reciting with a soft voice something I had written. "Here in Baghdad," he informed me, "We read all that is published in Beirut... I just proved it to you!"

❦

The new Gibelina stands like a memorial to the old. There's life to it, there's even more: celebrations, weddings, bells and musical events, but this moment in history is so bleak that the August Mediterranean sky appears to have the blue of an acid bath.

The bus is leaving Gibelina. Francesca is standing there, not quite awake it seems, glancing at the sky, then waving goodbye with a smile. There are only the two of us and the driver. We are nearing the sea. Afterward, we will turn right and follow the coastline.

Mind is mobile too, but unlike a vehicle set to go from one precise point to a well-marked destination, a human mind functions with billions of feelers, tentacles, laser-like beams. To use such a tool and try to follow it in all the directions that it can take all at once, one must be a fool, or be so shaken through one's foundations that nothing would stop one from trying the impossible. My mind is wandering too. We are on our way to Palermo.

Buland is wiping his face with a big handkerchief. I don't know if he's trying to sleep. He seems to be deeply sunk into his thoughts.

He came and sat near me. He declared that we were riding on a map and in a racing car, away from the army and toward a volcano. I was still feeling the throb of the previous night's party. I took the time to have a look at the scenery. The whole terrain was terraced and planted. The olive trees, with the mysterious beauty of their silvery leaves, were forming a new kind of a sea against the implacable Mediterranean. My mind was fast reconnecting with its kinship with weather and fire.

"Who built all these terraces?" he asked.

"Francesca told me that there are some sixty thousand Tunisian workers in Sicily and that they all are in the fields."

Buland immediately lost interest. He immersed himself in his private world. I could hear it, silently, feel its temperature, sense the physical pressure that it was applying on his brain. I noticed that he and his clothes were the same color. As for me, I was compelled to talk.

I mentioned the art show we had both viewed in Gibelina. I wanted to return to Pizzi Cannella's *Diary of a War*, to his immense paintings of burnt fields seen from beyond the sky, of targets pinned on grayish spots and always their titles: 1991, 1991…

I reminded him that we had stared a long time at the stone walls Cannella had covered with the visions of a war that was eating at his mind. He did not utter a sound.

I turned my head back to the window: Callefalsa, Sirignano, other little localities were signaled, as well as turn-offs to Balestrate, Trappeto… while the bus was pushing straight ahead.

ᦕ

The throbbing rhythm of the bus ride following the coast of Sicily loosened Buland's memories and he went on talking. At this very moment, so many years after, I still recall obsessively that fateful conversation.

"… Oh, yes, I'm a Kurd by the laws of ancestry, born in Ruwunduz, an eagle's nest on the highest cliffs of Kurdistan, but I'm an Arab, an Arab poet from Baghdad."

Pulling up his sleeve, he pressed his hand on his arm, and said that the Tigris was flowing through. At some point, his eyes narrowed and filled with compassion. "I have to love myself," he added, "I have to stop making my life miserable. London is a good place for Iraqis, we're numerous there. We see each other… but for what?"

As he came close to my face his forehead loomed big and balding. His clothes were used up, dark and uninteresting. He hadn't shaved but his voice was still soft and his speech careful.

I turned toward him as if we were sitting in a living room, to better hear him:

"I'm a man of the North fatally in love with a city that reaches 120° in the summer. A son of the North who threw himself in the arms of Tammuz, god of fire resurrecting.

"Touch here under my jacket. There's a heart there. It has been broken to pieces, first by my father, yes, that father who taught me pride from the day I was able to walk but who nonetheless beat me, beat me nearly to death. I had barely turned fourteen when one day he laid me on the floor, whipping the soles of my feet savagely, on and on. The whip was bloodied and my mother crying and screaming and he wouldn't let go. Then he made me stand on my wounds and slapped my face and you would have thought that that sound would reverberate through all the mountains of Kurdistan. A week later I was leaving town and on my sore feet I went from village to village all the way to Baghdad.

"My maternal uncle took me in. I worked at his

grocery store while going to school once or twice a week. I was reprimanded by the teacher. I was reprimanded by my uncle. My father gave me hell because, he claimed, he caught me kissing a young cousin who was visiting us. That was a lie. I had just pushed back a lock of hair hanging over her eyes and he saw me and madness struck. In that grocery store at least, each pound of lentils sold represented a pound of freedom acquired. Uncle Karim died with tuberculosis in his bones: in the summer people were used to sleeping on roofs, wrapped in sheets soaked in the river, to withstand the heat. So he mildewed like rotten fish.

"I returned home. But the curse of the family was still active. I always wonder why they wanted so badly that I be destroyed. Notice my wrists? They're scarred. They have something to tell, don't they? I was put in jail. Not because I was a communist, no, it happened much before Saddam exterminated them.

"Listen. My sister, the one a year older than me, was killed, yes, violent death is not always political. She was murdered by my eldest brother. That monstrous creature had raped her. But all that my family could think about was that the whole tribe was going to be dishonored if one day they found out. So they lied. They decided that they would declare that I was the one who had slit her throat 'because she had spent a night out of the house!' As I was then not yet legally an adult they knew I wouldn't be condemned for as many years as their eldest son would have. Their story sounded convincing to the tribal council, as well as to the central government authorities, which are trying to curb the recurrence of what are called 'crimes of honor'; and this the more so because I was in the habit of shouting to the wind that I was a poet. 'He's hot in the head,' my father repeated on and on; and, addressing the tribal council, he added, 'I must admit that he redeemed our honor.'

"The criminals I was imprisoned with taught me a lot. They turned out to be my philosophy teachers. Their thinking was always crystal clear. Not a single one expressed any remorse. They had to do what they did. That's all I heard. They explained to me that the moment of killing was a moment of supreme freedom. They were all believers. One of them reflected: 'I believe in God more than ever because once, for just one moment, I felt that I was God.' And that guy was the least violent of the group. When I asked him if he felt sorry, he, being rather soft-spoken, sweet, stared at me, then calmly answered my question:

"'Me sorry? For what? I grew up with anger, resentment, violence. Now I am quiet. I spent more than five years in this hole but it feels as if I have just arrived. My brother-in-law was tormenting the whole family, day after day. He used foul language with all of us. He was a mad dog. I had to stop him. When the knife entered his heart, my own heart was cleansed. What they called my 'crime' is what released my soul. I am free of hatred ever since.'"

Buland was perspiring heavily. He closed his eyes. Remained silent for a while, then resumed his narration:

"When I was let out of prison—I was there for one springtime—I went home. Nobody ever asked a single question."

ᵉᵗᵂᵉᵛ

"I knew Saddam closely. Yes, there was a period when I met with him often. Don't be surprised. He befriends poets and artists; he's an avid reader, too, showing in front of books the feverishness of a provincial adolescent. The written word has a magic hold on him."

Buland's voice slid into a monotonous rhythm. It had the slow speed of a stream running through private gardens, moving through a zone outside the perimeters of impersonal time.

"I loved Saddam and later I cried my eyes out for having done so. Shame was becoming unbearable. Until I escaped from the country, I had been eagerly listening to the tales of horror my friends in the Party were spreading around. They used to say how he started his ascension to power by participating in the assassination of Abdel-Karim Kassem. Whenever in front of him, I was transfixed. Always this fascination that people have for a murderer's hands. It is true that a man who has killed directly, has strangled, stabbed, or shot, should never reach a position of authority because, having once felt fear-less, above the law, all-powerful, he will need that feeling again and stop at nothing; at the same time, when demons will crawl all around paranoia will take hold of him, making him go from crime to new crime in order to cover up or justify his acts. A crim-inal act creates an addiction, a call for more, each crime soothing fears and creating grounds for new fears.

"I knew that Saddam was experiencing constant fever, thirst, insomnia, restlessness. I had many con-versations with him, but no, not about his politics and his obsession with crushing his enemies. There are many facets to that man's pursuit of grandeur.

"He funded yearly festivals that were held in the ruins of Babylon and to which literally some thou-sand poets were invited. Most of whom were there to praise his benevolence. I attended some of these gatherings and lost myself in the sea of words pronounced in so many languages. I was exalted, spellbound, and yet, gradually, I became apprehen-sive and disgusted.

"He looked so vigorous, so youthful at these events. His nervous energy made him radiant. He was cunning but had, still, a simplistic approach to things. One has to believe that power keeps one young. It keeps eyes alert, ideas bouncing, illusions flowering. But most of all, it keeps one lonely, disconnected. I was very young myself and the energy he was investing in millions of activities used to give the impression that the country was recreating itself. He has an instinct for mythmaking. He's also capable of courage. The danger comes from his deeply anchored conviction that he's a chief, a ruler, and therefore that he is the country, and that any harm to him will be disastrous to Iraq itself.

"His notion of power is primitive and tribal. And that makes him attractive for many in his land. He sees people as being either for him or against him. To that view of power, any opposition is simply treason.

"He is a supreme manipulator and in that sense, he is, in spite of what is said against him, supremely contemporary to the other rulers of the world. He was then as strong, and secretly as vulnerable, as a wildcat. Attentive, playful, capable of simplicity, able to befriend a beggar as well as an ambassador, he exuded self-assurance, even imperial generosity, although beneath it all hid an abyss of mistrust and a confusion that led him to make disastrous decisions in matters of war and peace, of life and death for Iraq. He created terror in order to silence the terror that was slowly but surely engulfing his soul.

"The magnetism that he exercises is, to a large extent, due to his self-absorption, which, too often, turns this basically ordinary man into a monstrous being, quick, unpredictable, and lacking restraint in the gratification of his impulses. Something is wanting in him, I used to think, and still do. He is animated by a perpetual hunger, a shapeless desire, so he goes on the prowl, and savagery brings him release as he throws himself frantically against the iron bars of a narrowing cage."

Buland moved a few rows ahead. I was succumbing to fatigue and my mind began to wander, mingling Sicily with the Arab East. Outside, the sea had turned into an immense blade of steel. I could rest neither my brain nor my eyes. The two had fused.

Buland returned and picked up his train of thought.

"I forgot to tell you that that crapulous being is an actor. A cheap one who can attract and subdue whoever comes near into a butterfly to the dark light that he is.

"I remember how one evening when a few of us were drinking with him, he stood, or rather stooped, as if he were carrying the world's burden. He looked as hard as God himself, for after all, didn't God have to be hard to chase the very first human beings he'd created out of the Paradise where they were having a happy life?

"You see, we identify power with the one who possesses it. People willingly become the prey of an abstraction personified. They worship their gods and worship the incarnate image of these gods. So many worshipped him. We can understand that: for a mouse, the only god he could worship would be the cat freezing him with fear.

"I hated myself for having loved that man. It still haunts me."

"Do you think that God died of excess of power?"

"For me God has never had a face. I joined the Party because I thought that it intended to transform our wretched reality into something better. Later I wondered if I had not succumbed to the solidarity offered by a militant group, with its seduction, its fervor, its certainties… otherwise, wouldn't everything be a mirage?!

"I rejected my father and then I did the same with the supreme One. God uses our miseries as a mask. He infiltrates the souls of the poor and makes them accept their condition. I had to settle accounts with both.

"You're listening. You have to. Somebody has to listen to me.

"It's over. I'm nothing. Sometimes I don't know if I think what I say, there's no affirmation in my poems, save my pain, which surges intact and follows me more closely than my shadow. At times I'm so alienated from my self that when I sign my name I wonder if I'm not committing a forgery. I don't know what to know. Every morning I'm not the same person who slept the previous night in my bed. I keep rolling, like earth in space. That man is watching. From far away, watching. He manages to torment our souls with his criminal mistakes, and when he doesn't kill directly, he sends his men to death, to war, and Iraq is on its knees, I am telling it to the world, we're in Italy, and it's sizzling hot over there, over there Tammuz is dying, the young god is dying and that man is alive!

"Indeed, there's decay all over. The school I attended is burning. The woman I love is turning to ashes in her grave. I warned her not to marry, but she did. They gave her away. I still want her; if I could want anything it would be her, the one they beat me for. I made love to many women amidst the smell of dates freshly cut from the palm trees, of fish frying in the kitchen, as well as on musty sheets in anonymous hotels, but I keep missing her, in each of the nights I ever spent with any of them I wasted my seed on her recurring image.

"The world has aged. God has aged. Monotheism is an old recipe, that's why fanatics have taken over. By repeating ad infinitum the sacred texts they emptied them of their substance. God's youthfulness has disappeared. He was immense and He shrunk. They're trying to give Him back His wings, but these are not taking off. An airplane bombing the hell out of a city is younger than God. Hiroshima is younger too. Look! I am forced to love planes, speed, terror!

"If God willed all that, if He indeed created us, He is then the one who gave Himself to us as a model of absolute power. And all that men have done ever since is try to equal that image, and therefore I will want to bring Him to judgment, to court, as Saddam one day will have to withstand trial and be judged."

The steady whirring of the bus was numbing me. Buland's last sentence was churning in my head: "I'm an obsessive writer, but who and where are my readers? Disseminated, beaten down, all of them beggars in one way or another. To write about them? Write about my misery, the Thames, a ridiculous royal family, Englishwomen?" My head was repeating, "Englishwomen," "Englishwomen."

***

The bus had gone beyond Villagrazie when the driver suddenly pulled by a gas station just off the road. He excused himself very gently. He had to have the vehicle checked as it was heating and making strange noises. "Take your time," he said, showing us a small table with two chairs.

I was happy to be able to stretch my legs. It was past lunchtime and I asked Buland if he was hungry. He did not answer. I plugged some money for iced tea into the vending machine, and sat holding my head in my hands. I needed some rest, I decided. Buland wandered around the building and then joined me. In the little store behind the bathroom he had bought a bottle of Chianti.

"It's too hot for wine," I remarked.

"Nonsense."

He uncorked the bottle. The driver was busy with two young men who were inspecting the bus and reporting to him. Buland was drinking. It was impossible to unwind while cars passed steadily.

Finally we climbed back to our seats. "We'll be in Palermo soon," shouted the driver.

Buland was a deflated mass of inertia. I wished he could sleep. For his own sake and mine. But a drunk poet is utterly unpredictable, I discovered. I read a sign that indicated a turn-off to Capati. The bus kept rolling. Buland started to sing, in Arabic, in Kurdish, in English… then he was humming, whistling softly, humming… a Kurdish lullaby, probably.

At last we arrived in Palermo. We had reservations at the hotel but Buland didn't follow me, didn't enter and didn't look back. He picked up his small suitcase and went.

The Master

I had this letter on my table for a while and finally I answered and accepted the proposition: a professor from Virginia had written to ask me whether we could meet when he would be in Paris for a couple of weeks.

The man is sitting in front of me in my spacious living room. He's a professor from the University of Virginia at Charlottesville in the Arab studies department. He asks my permission to record our conversation; I agree. He gives me his card with addresses, phone numbers, emails, and so on, none of which are familiar. He thanks me for having agreed to being interviewed. I don't feel particularly at ease, but if I said yes, it's yes. After all, why not?

He comes quickly to the heart of the matter:

he's gathering information on the Iraqi poets who lived during Saddam's era. He's done already a lot of research:

"I am sure you're the person I should see now."

"Well, if I can be of any help."

"I'm particularly interested in Buland al-Haidari's work."

"Have you read all of his books?"

"Of course. He's quite important for my project. I hope to do justice to them all, publish a book that will go beyond the usual academic stuff."

"They sure deserve it."

"You're a painter, aren't you? I noticed a painting of yours on the cover of a special issue of *Discourse*. It was a visual interpretation of one of Buland's poems, is that right?"

"Yes, that's a poem he wrote during the civil war on Beirut's destruction."

"Were you close to Buland?"

"I met him in Baghdad, then saw him quite often when he moved to Beirut. For a while we both lived there."

"When did you see him last?"

"Probably at the end of '93. Let me think. It must have been in January '94. That's it. A cold night in Paris."

"What was paramount on his mind then?"

"I remember that we talked about angels."

"Angels?"

"Yes, angels."

I would call that night the Night of the Angels.

Buland and I went to have dinner in a small neighborhood Italian restaurant to remind us of Italy. He had deteriorated much in the few years since Gibelina. He could have been taken for a bum, but at times he also looked beautiful. He got animated. Sparks were returning to his eyes. Between sips of wine he was trying to smile. Eventually, he did, and his face lit up, illuminated from within and not only by the candle that was burning on the table. It was a joyful meal; it was nice to see him eat, holding his fork in one hand while drinking with the other.

He offered to walk me back home and as it was damp and cold and we were close to the Seine, we hurried.

He lingered at my door and I noticed that he was being seized by some kind of a panic. I invited him to come in because he was also shivering.

"You don't have anything to drink?" he asked.

I pulled out a bottle of brandy. He hurried and took a big gulp. And right there and then, regardless of my weariness, of my need to be alone and go to bed, I had to bear the delirious rambling of his mind.

Did Buland live in a state of perpetual madness? Who knows? He was rather, probably, an unmapped volcano spewing flashes from his mind to one of the few people he could trust. He was not quite a person but something of a big bear from the forest, who wanted to show friendliness, speak on behalf of his particular species.

He went on with his brandy, quenching some bottomless thirst. Reluctantly, I tried to squeeze in a few words: "You're hurting yourself," I warned softly. But my remark unleashed a cataract of repressed anger.

"You're speaking like Zaha, you're trying to keep me alive! Why don't you people try to keep alive the millions of Iraqis who are unable to get medicine for their dying kids? To get clean water, a blanket in winter, shade in August. But they have sanctions! Iraqis are dying by punishment. Collective, radical punishment. Come on, all of you. Why should I live when everybody and everything is sinking, why?"

I covered his shoulders with a blanket, put a pillow under his knees, as he was sitting on the floor. He calmed down. I expected him to leave soon after but the relative rest that he felt launched him into a dirge-like disclosure.

"Sometimes a dreadful heat wave covers my face. That face is a mask, a mere skin. And whenever the mask breaks, when there's suddenly a hole which allows some imprisoned substance to bleed, to ooze out, the pain becomes hard to bear, produces a human earthquake; the self dissolves, the 'I' fades away and surrenders its space to madness. The collapsed container, my body, lies inertly, deflated, flattened. That's what I am. Don't call it a depression because I'm asking, who pierced the balloon, the mind, the heart, the stomach? I know who did it, I saw it: an angel!

"One night, that angel threw me on the floor, stepped on my body, and I didn't spit blood but my spirit, which is made of more sound than matter. He took possession of me. The good old self was gone. I became that angel. I'm who he was.

"I am a fallen angel, not Ibliss or one of his cohorts; I'm the greater for encompassing all the stations: those of the soul and those of the body; I transcend them all. The proof, if need be, is in my poetry. My poetry is the matrix of my destiny. I'm the prophet of my own destiny.

"Fire! I am fire. I'm a woman in love with Life's burning core. I'm that woman that I loved and lost the morning of our single night. I'm a living wound because I know that they're setting fire to my country because they envy its immemorial mystic power. It's the old story: their god took a chunk of clay and made a shapeless blob and blew into it his flaming breath: that turned his first two creatures into glass. And why did he make them transparent if not to better see through them? I don't deal with that being anymore. He is too cunning, the master of an ultimate technology. Too busy. Too busy. I need the invisible, I need purposelessness. I keep company with angels because they're fire. Fire has form while being immaterial. Air catches fire. Angels are invisible flames, they're existing spirits so long as they burn. I am interchangeable with them. But it is incredibly hard. Please help me keep in one piece!

"… Only angels are real. But angels don't last. They reproduce themselves by looking into a mirror and then they die; the reflection they see is a newly born angel. Their essence is dependent on their activities. They are supreme go-betweens, like poets. Like them, we are transient within Being and Being is transient."

⌒⋇⌒

The professor didn't comment. He just went to his list of prepared questions.

"Do you have any idea why Buland joined the Communist party?"

"The reasons must be obvious. It was a party for radical change."

"Didn't he know about the cruelties of Stalinism?"

"We never discussed it, but to be honest he must have."

"You like his poetry?"

"Yes, I do. I can't explain to you why, but his memory is particularly dear to me."

"We have something here."

A strange uneasiness warned me against this man that I had agreed to talk to.

"I'm sorry, I may be of not much use to you. He's dead now. I wish we could leave him alone. He was used to that. Why should we investigate people all the way into their graves?"

A cold fury took hold of my interlocutor as he was repressing his disappointment. He was not going to give up so soon. In the face of my reluctance, his eyes narrowed, his fists clenched. He brought his coffee to his mouth. After some small talk the conversation returned to the subject of angels.

"What did angels mean to him? Has he ever discussed the matter very seriously with you?"

"All I know is what his poetry says."

"This is one of my problems with him: how can a man who professes his atheism—with courage, I grant, in a profoundly God-centered culture—believe in the existence of angels? It doesn't make sense."

"If one reads him carefully one can see that he wasn't involved with beliefs but with vision. He wasn't interested in thought, either. We know that thinking is often no more than looking for ways to run away, cheat, cover up, transform or betray."

"You're all nihilists, aren't you?"

"We're all the contemplatives of an ongoing apocalypse. So what's left for us to think about… but are you a professor or an investigator?"

"Probably both… I am a Big Eye, the guardian of a supreme power. I don't need to believe in God, either, but I won't agree with you that these times are terrible. True, we have the means, and we are using them, to displace mountains. We have reduced some of them to powder, to dust, for example in Afghanistan."

"And turned Iraq into hell. What for?!"

"I can give you a lot of reasons. A book-length apology for our actions. But things are much simpler. We are running the world because we can. We have measured planets, sent probes to the most distant galaxies, so what if we destroy some evil countries here and there on this midget planet? We need no deity, no angels for that. You little guys are paying the price for it, right. You're the wood that keeps the fire going. There's no need to be sentimental. People will die anyway, one day or another. It's too bad if they happen to be in the wrong place. Somebody has to pay, somebody, and why should it be me? Let me tell you, you can burn all the philosophy books and the political theories. None of them reach the bottom of the truth and that truth is simple: the pleasure to kill is the greatest of pleasures. We made of history the justification of that pleasure. We made it glamorous. We ask little girls to kiss bombs that will be sent to smash other people's skulls. We love conquest and make it loveable. What do we love if not the sight of corpses run over by men riding horses, or lines of advancing tanks?"

He stopped, paced the room, drank some water, and went back to his chair.

"Anyway, the world can take it or leave it, we are recreating it on *our* terms."

I was hearing the tape recorder and it dawned

on me that in his suit and with his crooked smile, he must certainly have installed this same recorder in small villages, remote countrysides, on San Francisco's Washington Square, in Alexander Platz and the Taj Mahal, in the Nile Hilton, on top of Mount Everest, along the Rio de la Plata, and very probably on the moon.

The boss that he's serving is sitting on an arsenal of weaponry that could wipe out the world many times, although once would do. He knows it. He's enjoying it. He's getting his cues from a book in a language he ignores, but some of his advisors are ready to translate for him. It's an old book. It's not a gospel of good and evil, but rather the monumental description of a monumental desire: to own the world as one owns food in one's mouth. To eat and digest and expel from one's body the leg of a lamb darkly sacrificed. But for him, the lamb is you and me, human flesh tortured and thrown away in garbage bins.

What's his power? It's awesome, we know, but what is it?

It is the power to crush bones from a distance. Distance is of essential importance. It renders responsibility invisible and retaliation impossible. This power is multiplied by the ability to enter every conscience, to paralyze all impulses for curiosity or happiness, to silence doubt, to destroy any rebellion of the spirit, introduce self-censorship to the point of turning minds into mortal silence.

I was suffocating and needed some rest. I returned mentally to the olive fields of Sicily, remembered the sea and saw from a moving bus Tunisian workers taking a break under the shade. I needed to hang on to that reality.

The professor hadn't moved. There was a dark halo around his head. Then gradually, it was his head that went totally dark and white rays were radiating from it. I had to keep calm. I was only hearing a voice. A voice in the room was telling me, please, before we go any further into this poet's mind, listen to the basic premise on which America's power functions; it's the underlying thread of the world. You will understand who I am, and against whom Buland fought and lost, because he dealt with a primary concept, which is a key to all his thinking and is in my sense a basic flaw, I mean his notion of the nature of Time.

At this point the professor/agent went to the window and took a deep breath. He stood there silently. Then I think I heard him mumble to himself and say: "History, History! What a junkyard for the human race's stupid deeds!"

He turned toward me and stared. Then something prompted him to go to my bookshelves. He picked up one of Buland's books, looked for a particular passage and started to read aloud:

> Time does not reside in a watch. When
> you look for it, it has already moved, it

has already left. Oh yes, it has power! Transformed into a breeze, it makes love to water, second avatar of its intimate being. Thinner than the trace of a magnetic wave, it does not walk on things, it impregnates them. And when it runs out of patience, its dying dies.

Time is giver of existence. It flows through us or passes us by. It runs, gallops, decelerates, puts itself on full speed. It commands and energizes dictators. It runs, indeed. It takes the shape of a horse. Time is master of all.

Time did not create itself; it's not a creature. Time produces spirit. Spirit oozes from it as acidity comes from a lemon. Time is pure thought. Thought is not Time; it's a product, an artifact of the mind. Whose mind?

Time is mind, although no one's mind. It is its own is-ness. It oversees forests, hides in rivers: becomes the Nile, the Rhine, the Mississippi… it beats the measure for music, meanders in the slums' corridors. It is steam, it precedes destruction, it's the atom bomb, it goes beyond it, it's the DNA of the universe.

It is audible, like trains through cities and thoughts in the brain. It is hearing itself. It decays when we use it and when we decay it keeps going its immeasurable way.

It takes human shape and walks alongside as a visitor, a double, a Siamese companion. It penetrates dreams and functions best in that non-territorial realm. It spurts from the mind, which itself spurts from the body. But the mind is also its creation. Time gave the mind the tools it needs to make use of time, be one with it. And then, ultimately, mind gives up.

In moments of joy, time suspends its own traces. When we take power over time, in the void that surrounds it, joy resembles death, while it remains the opposite of death. Joy is a visitation that connects us to the gods and makes them become the citizens of Time. And their own leader whom we name God is still dependent on Time. But once in a great while, some privileged recipient, some mind, unites within itself God and time. The three become one, and that's Revelation.

"You must know," he went on, pleased with himself, "that what his likes and the rest of the world refuse to admit is that my country has defeated Time. We have conquered it. Annihilated it. We replaced Time with simultaneity, with omnipresence. We made of the present our empire. At this very moment our services are gathering information from all over the world; I mean we cover the world in its entirety.

Your poet doesn't believe in God. As for us, we believe in Him, but we don't need Him. At this very moment, our probes are nearing the core of the Big Bang, the beginning of beginnings. There we will go and in the ultimate particles of matter we will find our own image, in there, our birthplace and our end."

"Are you," I asked, "working on your project from such a perspective?"

"That's no perspective, that's reality. From where else can I start?"

"You're somewhere I am not. We're wasting our time. I suspected it, now I'm sure."

"Let me be clear, I want to probe souls as our machines probe space. We will sleep at peace only when no mind will keep a secret from us."

"You'll have plenty to do."

I turned on the television and together we watched the news. The announcer was speaking of the president's visit to Togo, an earthquake in Iran, a flood south of the Sahara; then, to my bewilderment, there was a debate on the burning of Baghdad's main library and the disappearance of its National Museum.

A line out of Walter Benjamin's *Theses on the Philosophy of History* shot through my mind: "… even the dead will not be safe from the enemy if he wins." Indeed, the constellation that we name evil has the will to destroy the human race and its habitat. That will is imparted to the men who run the world: total eclipse.

I was sure that the professor wouldn't contact me again, and I was relieved. But then, on his next visit to Paris, not long after the previous one, he was on the phone, suggesting that we meet just once more. I was annoyed but he insisted, he wouldn't relent, he said that he had just one more thing to discuss with me, one more question to ask, and I hesitated, I wanted to refuse, but I ended up agreeing. After telling him that the meeting should take place in a café, I made sure: "Please, no tape recorder this time."

We met at the Café de Flore's upper story. The place was empty of customers. Because it was summer, even the city was empty. We were alone.

Mister Professor was another man! He greeted me as if he barely knew me, as if our new encounter was for him a happy surprise. He controlled perfectly his voice's natural urgency.

"Would you believe that the Iraqi poet whom I had the honor to discuss with you has remained an enigma for the poor reader that I must be?"

"I think that poets are a mystery, but we nevertheless read them. Everything is a mystery, so why should we worry?"

"As you know, his writings show an overwhelming obsession with angels. Do you know of any other Arab poet as involved with angels?"

"I can't think of any."

"To tell you the truth, I can't figure out what he

really means by 'angels.' Such things don't make sense to me."

"Haven't you read the Scriptures? Haven't you studied Islamic thought? You must have."

"I read, I read everything! But where the hell did he get his ideas about these fluttering creatures… I'm serious. I do my best to really enter into his world."

I told him that he would never enter that world. But it was in his character to press on. I took great pains in explaining that poets dealt with the invisible. This last word brought out a burst of anger from him:

"The invisible is most dangerous. It's pure nonsense; still, one has to beware of it. The belief in it can be the unknown sign that can break up a whole book of equations. It can stop the machinery of the world."

He was pitiful. Against my own skepticism, I tried to steer the conversation toward a sensible discourse. But where to start? Paul Klee came to my mind. I assumed that he was familiar with his paintings.

"I'm familiar with Rilke," he informed me, "but have seen very little of Klee."

"In World War I, when enlisted in the army, Klee was assigned to paint airplane wings. After the war he devoted himself to the task of changing the world through art, as you know… The advent of World War II threw him into a panic. He returned to his preoccupation with angels. While he was disintegrating in his body, literally drying up, he had a series of visions of angels that he recorded, made visible, in drawings and paintings. Their ominous presence constituted an avalanche: *Archangel*, *Angelus Militans*, *Vigilant Angel*, *Angel Overflowing*, *Angel from a Star…* they kept coming."

"I don't read paintings. I am a philosopher."

"Then you must have read Walter Benjamin."

"Yes. Of course. There was a crazy professor in my youth who made us read him thoroughly. But these books never made sense to me. They are rather subversive, the very opposite of what we need now. We need positive thinking."

"Buland was extremely familiar with his works; he had read everything he could find translated into English. Anyway, the Arab poets that you are studying are too alien to your worldview, aren't they?"

"Your Walter Benjamin is dead."

"You mean?"

"He moves on the orbit of revolutions, looks through the dark prism of his romantic pessimism, stirs up the poor and the vanquished… the very terror that we are fighting against."

"There are realms for which only poets have keys. If you reread him carefully, you will understand what I mean."

The professor remained silent. Then he remembered:

"Oh! Do you say this because somewhere Benjamin mentioned some famous angel painted by Paul Klee… is that the connection?"

"You're right. But it's not just a connection, it's an affinity between them. Angels speak to each other, exactly like poets. I believed, when we met, that you wanted to listen to them."

"Listen? To whom? To the poets or the angels? We're on different planets. I deal with information. I deal with things, like this table, this cup, this waiter over there. Or with sentences that are coherent."

"But angels are information. Otherwise, why should you bother with your research? I've told you that. I'm sorry. There may be plenty of them in this café where we're sitting, how do we know? If you spend a night alone in this place, you might see some… You're looking at me with such contempt for what I'm saying. All kinds of realities may inhabit a place together… who are we to tell?"

"Well, I don't need to buy any of this. But tell me more. You're right, in a way. It might be useful to figure out how a strange mind like Buland's functioned. I've wondered many times how I've allowed myself to be entangled with this whole line of work. They're all lunatics. I suspect, though, that we still have to break the code to their thinking. Nothing must be overlooked, even if the people to whom I will report are already saying that all this crap is not worth their pennies."

"You would be surprised by what they can understand. They're themselves the darkest of angels, keepers of the underworld."

"This is not a conversation. I should excuse myself for having bothered you with this project of mine. We're getting nowhere."

My thoughts had acquired a momentum that was too hard for me to stop. I went on recollecting, and explaining how Benjamin had focused on one of Klee's most famous angels, the *Angelus Novus*, which he found, and I think acquired, in the early twenties. For the German poet/philosopher, that was the angel of history, "that visionary angel [who] is seeing the chain of catastrophes which affected humanity as the unfolding of a single and continuous event."

But I would think that when Klee drew that angel, he endowed him with the totality of his metaphysical vision. That angel is not only the angel of history but also the angel of the future, a future whose cataclysms will continue and surpass those of the past.

We can say that when he's staring at history he is also staring beyond, at cosmic destiny. Hadn't Klee, in the "Creative Credo," his earliest piece of writing, and about the time he was painting his *Angelus Novus*, written: "I seek a place for myself only with God. I am a cosmic point of reference… I cannot be understood in purely earthly terms"? That angel must have been for Klee both a self-portrait and the depiction of an angelic principle that resided within him as well as being autonomous and independent of Time.

"*Angelus Novus*," I went on telling the puzzled professor, "is figured in the painting as a wild beast with a leonine face, the wings of a bird, the feet of a bovine, and with atrophied wings ending with human hands at their extremities. He is a composite figure that calls to mind the winged creatures that guarded the Babylonian temples, and also suggests a living tree. This all-encompassing form embodies, at once, the journey of Being from cosmos to plant, to animal, and to man-the-angel. It is also a link to the past because although it announces a being for the future, it fuses the emblems of the four Evangelists into a single image. It is Klee's ultimate creation of Parousia—of Revelation.

"*Angelus Novus* is the *new* angel because he is neither one of the contemplative angels who are in perpetual adoration of God, nor a messenger. He is himself the 'good news.' He is not only propelled by a storm, but is himself the storm. We don't need eyes to distinguish him but ears. He is the prototype of the poets (poet/philosophers, and artists) who will deal with these destitute times. That's what poets are for: to be the energy, to take part in the perennial physical and spiritual battles waged for the destiny of man. That action is always urgent, although the outcome of these confrontations has been and always will be, throughout the centuries, open-ended, precarious, and this, until end's end."

৵৵

For days I felt disturbed by my latest encounter with the "inquirer" from Virginia. But as I took the firm resolution of not meeting him again, come what may, I began feeling relieved of the dark cloud that his presence had left behind.

And one night I had a dream and in that dream I heard Buland's voice. It wasn't clear where it was coming from. The voice asked me imperatively "to take a pen and write"… and Buland appeared, and simultaneously lightning crossed the sky and then it was night again. His apparition lingered, a cloudy and white substance quivering in that obscurity. His face was blacked-out, his features were gone, only the vague shape of a body and a voice seemed recognizable. I found myself in an aviary full of shrieking birds. Though I couldn't see them, I was aware of being surrounded by their frantic movements. Then the whole scene vanished and here was Buland, a voice omnipresent coming from all directions, and he was informing me that his angels had betrayed him. "They are devouring me," he was shouting, "they are starting to take my skin off, I am the meat of their banquet, which is being held by the Tigris, in the City of the Balance."

The Power of Death

I t was raining hard when he came to see me and we both looked through the windows and commented on Paris's summers: hot, and so often wet, and we agreed that they have a way of breaking one's heart as if for no apparent reason. We tried to talk about something cheerful but somehow everything seemed bleak and we gave up. We looked at each other, and we could have been lovers, but we had been friends for so long that the air between us was always standing still.

I will call him Wassef, because that's the name he should have had, don't ask me why.

While the rain stopped and the sky remained dark I made him a cup of coffee. I tried to put on the radio for some music but he showed such displeasure that I stopped searching for a good station. He told me, in the form of a question, that he was on his way to Stockholm. "Do you know that I'm going there?" he asked, and went on talking.

Suddenly I was sure that he was going with the single purpose of looking for Erica, and I didn't speak much. It rained again, and then the sky lifted, just a bit, just a shade, and we couldn't find things to say, and eventually he left, leaving the door slightly open. I had no reason to cry but I did.

I later learned from him that he searched frantically for Erica and couldn't trace her and that, just when he was resigned to go back to Damascus, he received at his hotel a note from a relative of hers whom he had contacted, telling him on a little piece of ordinary paper scribbled with a black pencil that Erica had died, exactly two weeks before his return to Stockholm.

Wassef's tone of voice over the telephone belonged to a man who was close to losing his mind. "Come back to Paris," I suggested, "and let's talk it over." He went on rambling and for one long hour he reviewed the main events of his youth. Yes, he studied in Sweden, and met Erica when they were at the university; yes, they discovered love together, and she was a virgin when at the end of his first year at the school of engineering they went north, and didn't sleep for days and made love as if outside the hours, with the curtains drawn, their bodies quivering with fatigue and happiness.

One would think that there is nothing new to love stories, but Wassef was recalling his life with such intensity that the world was being created anew through his pain, although sinking also into an abyss of frightful proportions.

I knew that he had left Erica when he got his degree, returned home, and eventually got married. But his wife had died in childbirth and he remained in his parents' house where they helped him raise the child. He used to come to Paris quite often, but had never returned to Sweden.

His voice over the phone was hard to bear, his sorrow was too cruel; in fact it seemed that cruelty itself was hurrying in through the windows until I felt I would suffocate. I begged him to come immediately so I could be reassured while taking care of him. "Don't worry," he said, "I'll write you a letter." He hung up.

As I knew him too well, I filled in the spaces of his life. He convinced himself, for years, that he had forgotten Erica, as he never liked to burden himself with feelings of guilt. He also had some excuses: for years his country had experienced incredible upheavals; revolution and repression had been his daily bread for so long that he never allowed himself the luxury of a past. And now, like a door slamming in his face, the past was catching up with him.

His letter arrived: *I am walking through transparencies night and day, and each time I stop I discover a particular moment of the life I had with Erica.*

Sometimes she walks near me, as she used to, and the sun creates shadows under her eyelashes and she looks at me, a bit later, stares at me while we sit face to face to have lunch, and in the afternoon she lies on our bed and she takes her time and then we lose ourselves in each other and I carry her voice within me and I hear it now telling me she loves me and I believe her, now more than I ever did, but then I know she died recently, as her cousin wrote me, and I refuse to go to her tomb because I'm afraid to imagine the state of her body in there, and it is hot and luminous outside while I write you this letter, but I have to tell you that she just came in and she's playing with my hair and the smell of her body is filling the place and it's overwhelming me and I may faint any moment as I may also never send you this note.

But listen. Never in my life have I felt that I could lose control of my reason but I do now because her life and her death are mingling and I don't know where she really is, if she's hiding somewhere on this earth or if she's really dead; then where is she and would I ever find her if I died too, but this universe is so big, so vast, so out of reach in its infinite dimensions, where would I have to go to follow her and find her and see her once more, a minute, a second, a fraction of a second, once, just once, even if she has to appear as a ghost and frighten me and fill me with bliss, or come under unbearable lights or in the deepest darkness that my eyes and my mind could sustain.

His letter went on and on, becoming utterly desperate, bringing no order to his emotions or thoughts. Often he was delirious, mixing the present with the past, speaking of hallucinations, threatening suicide. He also described the weather, carefully, obsessively, the Swedish summer he remembered and the one he was again experiencing. Here, in Paris, the rains were hot, as if the skies too could be irrational, and I read and reread his pathetic words.

He called again, asking me to go and see him, saying, "I need somebody here who can understand the pain I'm going through. I need you. I really do."

I turned in circles in my flat, went to the Luxembourg Gardens, drank coffee after coffee… I had no choice but to go to Stockholm. I phoned and left a message at his hotel, booked a room at the same address and made a plane reservation, giving myself one more day in Paris before my flight.

I am one of those people who still link Sweden with Nordic legends and black-and-white movies, although the night before I left, I went to the Champollion and saw *Niagara*, that old Marilyn Monroe flick that throws together a lot of water, passion, and doom. There were many close-ups of Marilyn's face and I wondered if each of her films was not about her own destiny. She played her own role, I thought, until fiction became real, and she left behind her the image, repeated ad infinitum, of our own impossible loves. It wasn't planned as such, but it was the real beginning of my trip.

I won't say that I was happy to find myself in Stockholm so suddenly. Wassef is dear to me, yes, I was worried and eager to see him, but travel in the European summer has about it something deflating: Europe is European in winter, it always seems. Since early childhood in Damascus, I viewed Europe as a land of gray skies and frozen fountains, the nights shining with electricity. But what of Stockholm in the summer? A city that sizzles in a country considered cold, a no man's land subverted by melancholy, the monstrosity of sunshine on the heart's deserts.

My hotel room was comfortable, but Wassef was absent. He had left a note telling me that he would be back soon. He didn't say what he meant by "soon," a few hours or much longer.

I waited. I turned on the television but other than the Grand Prix Formula One races, there wasn't much I could understand. Of course there was the news, and I could watch what I already knew. The Grand Prix was fun: it got my mind off Wassef for a few laps. Schumacher won the race and there was his trophy, followed by Germany's national anthem. The guy who came in second was utterly miserable. The whole thing was taking place in Belgium while it was raining, the cars sliding. It all looked like science fiction but it was real, for all that reality's worth.

I had lunch, then dinner, at the hotel's coffee shop. I tried to read Michael Sells's work on Ibn

'Arabi—I'd been in the middle of the chapter on the Garden among the flames before I left Paris—but it was useless; my peace of mind had been shattered. I drew the curtain tightly and tried to sleep, but light continued to seep through. I remembered past enervations but that was no help. I knew that I was in the middle of an endless luminosity and that the day was stretching on until midnight, ending where the next one was waiting... I didn't sleep the next day either, and the third went by, anxiety filling my time like rising water. I couldn't even get myself to be mad at Wassef and return home.

One late afternoon, a knock on my door. Wassef was back; he stood before me haggard, crazed, shaking, the whole of his being engulfed in some irradiating darkness that was made particularly conspicuous by the extra glare of light his entrance brought into the room.

Oh, why did he arrive in such bad shape! He didn't excuse himself for his absence, didn't ask if I was worried, or angry with him. He remained in his own world without making the slightest effort to reach out. He smelled of alcohol and sweat and the odor of defeat. After a moment I said, "Wassef, please sit down on this chair," but he paced the room, alternately opening the curtains, looking out, and closing them, until I asked him again, this time more firmly, to take a seat. At last he sat down on the bed, took off his shoes, then his jacket. He was wearing a pink shirt that I shall never forget, because it had something charming about it and for some other reason I couldn't define.

"Please, keep the light out of this room," he begged, and remained silent afterward. I drew the curtains together as closely as I could and lit the lamp, but the electricity was useless, for we were sitting in an endless twilight.

"Where were you?"

"Nowhere."

"I am here for you, to help you, if you need me."

"I never need anyone."

"Well, I'm here, we can talk."

"I have nothing to say."

…

"No, it's not true. I will need a lifetime to repeat it again, to say it all, and I can't, of course… Do you believe I ever had a life?"

"Wassef, try to answer your own question."

"Yes, I had a life, I have one, and it's miserable; I'm probably going mad and I don't know it."

"You're not in any danger, I would think. Just tell me where you've been these last days and then we'll start."

"Start what?"

"This story of your life."

"My life ended long ago," Wassef said, "long ago, the day I decided to go back to Damascus, but I didn't know it, it took me a lifetime to realize that

I was dead, a ghost seemingly happy. Erica cried and she was sweating, her hair all wet, her face as under pouring rain, and she was looking at me intensely, and kissing my face, falling into a deep silence, and then weeping, again and again, like a newborn animal, and then everything stopped while I felt paralyzed, wondering if I would ever get out of that room, that tiny space in which I had experienced incredible happiness, a sort of bliss that used to turn into a warm current feeding my veins, and her skin was soft under mine, and her breathing even, soft like her voice, and I was lost in her hair, and in between her lips, and my heart was beating, it was a messenger bringing good news, and her legs were long and smooth and always warm and, even in the dead of winter, she was burning and radiating a slow, steady fire, and here I was, pulling myself away from it all and her own blood was receding toward her chest and she looked pale and her breathing was becoming difficult and I started looking at the door and she understood that it was over, for no reason, it was all over for her, and for me too, and I don't know how I went through that door never looking back, never to see her again."

It was obvious that something had broken down within Wassef, so I had to sit and wait and listen to this old friend, this man who was racing back to his youth, erasing some forty years of his life in order to reach the two or three years of intense happiness he'd experienced, Erica's death broke his will to pieces,

and the deeper truth that he had hidden so success-
fully from himself was shining now to shattering
effect. He'd never stopped loving her, but it took her
ultimate disappearance for him to come back to her.

Tension was high, to say the least. As the noose
of his anguish tightened around me, I decided to go
out for a while, take a walk. I asked him to stay and
wait for my return or go to his own room, but he
remained numb. I opened the door, went down a
couple of flights and met the street with relief. I came
to a corner café and gulped down two tall mugs of
beer, soon realizing that it was the last thing I should
have done, as the beer reinforced the effect of the
gray luminosity that was sticking to the walls.
Instead I drank some more, thinking it would help
me sleep.

When I got back, I found my friend spread out
on my bed. He was barefooted, with his shirt unbut-
toned, staring at the ceiling. He didn't move when he
heard me come in. Suddenly, like a snake, he threw
a question, startling me: "We only see things that
don't exist, don't we?"

He went on: "Now I know for sure that I won't
lose her again. In her solitude, she is mine, all mine,
forever, like before, years ago, as if it were yesterday,
and that she's here, in this room, facing me, then
moving around, yes, Erica, we shall go to Uppsala,
do you remember the summer we went, sometime in
June, you are in Queen Christina's palace, that gray
hall we visited, and you're sitting on the throne and

I am the ambassador from Syria, I brought you perfume and dates, you will wear the one and eat the
others, and everybody knows I love you, they're
looking at us, and then we went to our hotel room,
we made love, and I tried to do it again, you told me
you were too exhausted by the trip, the heat, the
light!, but I tried again, I thought that would help
you fall asleep and you were fighting the light and
got nervous, and so did I, and we started to turn on
our bed and you made little sounds and I was fighting some invisible element, it was the light
intensified behind the shutters, pressing itself, and
you were burning with fever, begging me to stop
because you loved me, and loving me was enough,
and we didn't need to make love on and on when
she could barely breathe, and my own energy had
been spent, and our eyes would stay open, and then
I put my head in the hollow of her neck and tried to
rest and she laid her hand on my back and we were
outside the limits of time in a country with a never-
ending summer that wears out its lovers as if they
were meant to be doomed.

"And listen, listen to me, I left her. I ran away. By
the end of that summer, when nights started to
return to relieve us of the sun's power, when things
had a chance to brighten up, I told her, with no
warning, like a thief, a coward, a traitor, that I was
leaving the very next morning for home. That night,
while making love, she cried, and didn't say a word
but kept quivering, she didn't kiss me but remained

placid like the sea's surface on an August morning; then she stopped crying and looked at me for a long time, for ages, and she got up before me, earlier than usual, not having slept, she dressed, made coffee, I ate and she didn't, didn't even take a sip from her cup, and a few hours later I found myself on a boat, and she was standing on the quay, and then I never saw her again."

"And now," I interrupted, "You're back, after all these years, or where are you, why did you suddenly think of her, what triggered all this pain, these memories?"

"These are not memories!" he shouted. "You must realize that the past has come back, that she is here in front of me, she loves me and she's my universe, the whole of it… But no! I will never sit facing her, laughing, drinking in her presence, abolishing anything that is not her.

"I am today the man I should have been, now that the walls of the kingdom have fallen down and that she's invisible to all but myself; yes, I was receiving all these messages she kept sending these last years, telling me that she would die and give this Earth back to its wretchedness.

"But what did I do? I lied to myself. I looked for women, intensely, taking advantage of the travels that my work required, in many European capitals I paid women to spend nights with me and thought I was satisfied, until that night in Berlin, about a year ago, when I picked up a young girl of the age that

Erica had been when I left her. The girl was new to the streets, shy, embarrassed and rather disarming. I don't know why I kept asking her during the whole night to repeat that she loved me. 'Please keep telling me that you love me,' I begged, and she kept saying it in German, then I taught her to say it in Arabic; she said it, then reverted to German... and she fell asleep. In the morning she told me I was a strange fellow and that it should have been obvious that she couldn't love me, like that, just like that, and when I told her that I knew that but I needed to hear that sentence so that something in me could believe it, or half believe it, she kissed me gently on the forehead, refused to take my money and left. An hour or so later I gave the money to the woman who came to clean the room and she thanked me many times, and I tried strolling aimlessly in the streets but nothing worked, then I dealt with my business and returned to Damascus convinced that I was a man destroyed."

I tried to distract him and suggested that we take a walk, but he complained about the persistence of the summer light, then I said let's go and see a movie, and that suggestion turned out to be disastrous. He plunged deeper into a world all his own, his voice trembled and he continued:

"There was in the Damascus of my childhood a movie theater, do you remember, where you had to go down a few stairs? In there, since I was twelve or so, I used to enter a universe of beautiful women, they were not just women, but magic, unattainable, private, all to myself. I saw Jean Harlow, then Marlene Dietrich—the most impressive ones—they were blond, as silky as the river's surface, and I would come home with fever then take one with me in my bed, they were the first women I had, I made love to the most enchanting images in the world, and I would cling to my sheets, which were as smooth as the screens on which they appeared and disappeared, and they were haunting me in the classroom, their pictures hiding in my books. The world was full of them, I was telling myself, I will grow old and travel and join them, which one I don't know, but it will have to be in a place like in the movies, with stairways, moonlight, music playing in the background and stopping when we kiss. Then I did leave, with a scholarship for Stockholm.

"When I met Erica she belonged to the movies, she created an atmosphere overheated with tension, the promise of unending nights and surrender, and this became true, my dreams granted as to no one else. Her body had a horse's madness, she would smile and her smile would change the weather, draw me in… And one day I gave her up, for what, I don't know. I would give anything to know what really happened, in which one of my soul's layers… I buried myself in Damascus, entering the pitiful routines of visits to whorehouses in Madrid, Hamburg, Amsterdam, cheap versions of my childhood cinemas, then worrying about such things as train schedules and business appointments, even forgetting that I was still alive."

Wassef couldn't cope with himself. Sweating heavily, getting red in the face, he was becoming incoherent. His monologues were signals of such desperation that they made me slide and sink into a strange sadness made of sympathy and fear, and my inability to absorb his pain made me feel hard and inadequate. At some point I managed to persuade him that he had to return to his room, and I remember the panic I saw in his eyes. He turned his back, opened the door and moved his heavy frame out and down the stairs.

The next day I called him and there was no answer; the reception desk informed me that he had gone out quite early but that his belongings were still in his room. I was happy that he hadn't checked out. That same day I decided to return to Paris and wrote him a few awkward lines to let him know that I had to leave and that he could always contact me at home as usual. I did feel a bit shameful. I was running away. I tried to believe that by having stayed a couple of weeks in Stockholm, for his sake, I had done all that I could and hoped that he would follow me to Paris, or return to Damascus now that there was nothing he could do, nor anyone he could see with whom he could talk about Erica.

Once in France, not a day went by without my trying to reach him. He was not there. One day, at last, I was told that he had come by his hotel that very morning, took his baggage and left; they had no further information. I felt utterly cut off. The summer, I thought, had indeed ended.

Then one dismal and rainy morning I found a letter from Wassef in my mailbox. It was posted from Stockholm and written with a troubled hand. I went up to my apartment, waited for a while, tried to do a few things, make some calls, wash some dishes, put some music on, but nothing would alleviate my confused fear of this unopened envelope… Then, I read it:

Dear, dearest, I'm here, and you're my only friend, you know it, you've known me for so long, you remember the days when Damascus still had a river, and we loved it, it was a galloping torrent in the spring, and now they've covered it with the same kind of cement that covers their souls, but my own soul, where is it, where? Do I still have one, who am I? I have to speak with you about Erica, you'll understand. Since her death everything is so clear, crystal clear; her death has brought an excruciating clarity upon the world and now that I know she isn't here, it's late, always too late, it's useless, I know that only love matters, absolutely so, and how can I tell her that she freed me, she took my lies away with her death, that now I can love her, as she did then, she loved me as I love her now, and I'm hurling my head against a wall, her absence is a wall, and I'm breaking myself against it. Dearest, I'm suffering beyond anything I ever knew, beyond what one can bear, the world is flat and silent, there's so much light, this dead light of Sweden, which is unbearable, I am alone with her and she's a ghost, lying there in her tomb, starting to rot, and they wouldn't tell me where she's buried, I won't touch that tomb anyway, I will have to have it opened, it will make her death real, it would, it's as well that I don't know where she is, she's everywhere, here, in my head, my eyes, in front of me, once in a while she comes in my sleep and never stays for long, and I am given back to her absence.

I have to let you know something I did, in an ultimate effort toward total illusion, and at this point I can't understand if I'm a monstrous being, if I've always been a wicked failure behind what people called my gentleness, but we have to come to the point where we know who we are and why we've done whatever we've done, and if it could have been otherwise, where did everything go wrong, or is it rather that things had to be what they have been and in both cases it's terrible, it's maddening, I could have had a long life with Erica, come every night to her bed, her body, her presence, her luminosity, and I lost her by my own doing… Good God, was it impossible from the beginning, given who I was, a young man with no sense of the future, no means to think other than of the passing moment, tied down by ancestral timidity, and defeat must have been inbuilt in me if I had to turn my back on the only happiness that I had ever experienced?

I want you also to know something of the nightmare I'm going through now. You see, when this love for Erica resurfaced, engulfed me, it possessed me with such force that one afternoon, when I saw myself in the mirror, I looked young again, with the face I had when she and I were together, clouds and turmoil crossed my eyes, women were staring at me in the street and I felt that I could conquer any of them, as I did for a period of my life, and I found out that it is precisely because you are madly in love with a woman who is absent that you can most likely say yes to any other adventurous one, thus desire becomes a fire that will burn any piece of wood, and that happened. I met a young woman while I was at the coffee house; she was sitting at a table next to mine. She smiled and I answered her call, I was feeling young again and we walked aimlessly until dinner time, but the summer light lingered on, and getting tired, I invited her to come to my room and she accepted, and then it happened, I enveloped her with my desires, my passion for Erica appeared to her to be meant for her, and I let the poor girl believe it because I needed to believe it too, and we made love furiously.

I moved in with her, she was going to the university and I waited all day, dreaming simultaneously of two women, mixing their images, and sometimes crying.

For the first time in my life I felt grateful, unreservedly, allowing myself to be disarmed, but I didn't let my heart feel sorry for this young person to whom I knew I would never give much of anything and I wasn't embarrassed to be living an imposture.

Things just happened, instant after instant. I was watching her when I noticed some stormy ocean inside her blue eyes and a broad smile breaking on her face for no reason whatsoever, and she was moving her head on the pillow, pushing back her hair without touching it; then I became a traveler on an unknown highway, at an intersection I took a side road and I was with Erica again, looking for her under the skin of my new conquest, it was both awful and exhilarating, I thought that a dream of resurrection could only be fulfilled by death, the death that had already happened, it was all over, and possibly something else would break through, a disclosure, the resurrection of time, the repetition, the sacred repetition of what had been sacred. New ideas rushed forth, they interfered, they required an answer. I wondered if in the past Erica had done anything to have inhibited me which I had stored in my mind's deepest recesses. Was it possible that she had been the source of a desperation that I felt and never formulated, did she make me sense from the beginning that our relation was transient in essence, seeking an absolute with no roots in this world? Must I bear my guilt alone?

But it's true, it's true that she loved me desperately, totally, as a cloud loves another cloud and merges into it, why must I keep playing a game, now, when I'm under her death's absolute power, having lost the very notion of my own self?…

Yes, we went dancing one late evening, the air was motionless, the sky a canopy of fog and indifference. We found a little bar where youngsters were drinking and there was a jukebox and I found an old tango and we danced while I was aware that the young people were sneering at us, at my grayish hair, and then a small miracle happened, I found an old American song that used to be Erica's favorite, a smashing success back in the fifties, it was "Kiss of Fire." She often danced alone to this tune, with such independence in her body that I went crazy with envy and desire while she was moving, sure of herself, enjoying her power over me. But my partner was hearing this music for the first time and she liked it because it seemed to please me. We danced some more, and came home, and I watched her eyelashes, which at a certain angle made shadows on her cheeks, and her eyes looked as if through a veil, and I wondered if she wouldn't give me at last the illusion that Erica was alive, between my hands, just for a while, just for me, even if it had to be only for a fraction of a second.

The next day I bought her a dress, a deep blue silk dress with little flowers on it, and in the evening I gave it to her and asked her to wear it; she giggled and looked beautiful, and we went out and drank a lot when something suddenly upset me, and we hurried home. Once in bed I fell asleep immediately and dreamed of doors which remained closed while dead fish were being unearthed from a patch in the garden that my grandparents owned in Damascus. The following day my body kept shaking not with fear but with apprehension, I tried to eat lunch but had just coffee with a cheese sandwich, and felt old. Then I was seized with the frantic desire to find the perfume Erica used to like. I needed *it, it was oceanic; I searched in many stores; a French perfume quite famous in the old days, our days. I found out that it was still on the market, the salesgirl looked at me strangely, and I bought the little flask and waited impatiently. That evening I gave it to my little girl-friend, my mistress, she said, "What's this?" I replied that I had just bought it casually, and I lied by telling her that I was eager to discover its smell.*

I opened the bottle. I could as well have opened a tomb. I sniffed. The perfume seemed neutral at first, then it spread and made me feel disoriented, dizzy. It was a bit nauseating. When she rubbed some drops on her skin I entered Erica's smell as one enters a chapel—or a vortex—and this young woman smiling at me was not aware that I was using her to recapture a ghost. I pushed her onto the bed, my urge becoming violent, confused, I was at once unspeakably happy and desperate. I had entered again the chaos of love, its matrix, holding my breath and breathing it, holding under me a woman who was real and alive while I was making love to a phantom, until that absence mingled with the present to recreate the primordial night… My eyes closed, their lids fused, so that I could see that resurrection was happening, that I was recovering my sense of ecstasy… Erica's body was pulsating like neon lights all over mine, as well as over my young lover's, and I was aging over this perfumed and innocent body which in my mind was being mixed, gradually and irrevocably, with emanations of death.

I was begging my salvation from this abused woman. I poured more perfume on her, renewing an old addiction, trying to recapture the state of bliss I used to know with Erica, wishing that Erica be there, and mine, for one night, at least, and I called "Erica!," and the young girl shook me off her body and cried out loud with bottomless anger that I was now taking even her name away from her, and giving her one which wasn't hers, but all I knew with burning clarity was that Erica was lost forever, that time had indeed lapsed, that I was only an old man with a knowledge now so useless that it had to be thrown away, and I came close to killing her. I think I did it, within the smell of death, sniffing like an animal and pressing hard at the top of her breast, at her neck's tender line, I was pressing so hard that her face was obliterated from my sight, I was sweating and licking her perfume which was turning sour, I couldn't tell if my young victim was sleeping forever, as Erica was already doing, having preceded her with her immobility and decomposed body I was learning with that same unbearable clarity that to kill is just another way of crying, blood replacing tears.

My dearest, I could go on and on with this letter, even if it were only to postpone the moment when this will be over, this conversation with you, this agony. Listen, I told you that I won't visit her tomb, but there's no tomb for her, that's what I learned recently, it's hallucinating, they took her away from me, for sure, they cremated her so that I can never find her, never, and so many forces are fighting in my head, all of them invisible, so I don't see why I should go on living... and still, I am in a state of prostration and while you read this letter I may very well be under arrest, or thrown into a world lonelier than a prison cell, hopelessly devoid of any horizon. Yes, all threads are broken, the tiniest ones too; we'll have total darkness again. I'll remain in this city for a while at least, getting out of my hole just to prowl the night. There must be a wisp of smoke, some particle of hers that I can breathe, they burned her and her fumes will be eaten by me, swallowed, made one with my flesh, I will descend, Oh God, help me if you exist!, I am not Orpheus but I will follow her, somewhere, and she won't be there, I know, I'm sure, but I'll keep searching. She used to call me her baby, but that baby died long ago, as will the old man I am now, the sooner the better, here, or in the underworld, I'll drown in my sorrow, I don't know, I don't want anything, I can hardly move, but I will stay although I'm already left with nothing, I mean nothing.

I went through his letter and my brain sucked its own blood, I reread it, then I opened the window, later read it again… and Paris was soft and in the dark, a thin rain was wetting the air and I phoned Wassef's old hotel, I needed some connection with Sweden, with him, but was told that they hadn't heard from him for quite a while, and, just to add something, I asked about the weather and they told me it was still fine. Anyway, I know that the summer is over and that the Swedes are about to start their long descent into winter and its uninterrupted darkness.

The American Malady

I am in Paris, bedridden. My eyes, as tired as my soul, try to follow one cloud after another, when there are any. Paris's sky is particularly sealed, in imitation of the iron safes of its banks or the iron curtains which, in little Arab towns, fall over the front of the stores on Fridays and Sundays. The radio is on my left, the door a little further down. Facing me is the window. War is in Beirut and sorry is everywhere.

There have not been spectacular suicides in Paris. To the contrary. Arab refugees settle here, or prepare diplomas. In ten years, one Lebanese out of two will have a Ph.D. and the other will have nothing. But no Lebanese will still have the eyes he or she had before the war. Their eyes now express hardness, or the void.

Everything makes "news" nowadays. Newspapers, television, the radio, all follow events the way a hunting dog follows the game and bring back in its muzzle a dying bird. And people have never been as little informed as they are now. Camel caravans were much more reliable lines of communication than the stupid reporting that allows three minutes for an earthquake, a few seconds for the landing of a Saudi king, a minute and a half for the bombing of an Iraqi nuclear power plant, a bombing that in real time took twenty seconds. The entertainment goes on. On nights when on Channel 4 or 5 nobody dies in Somalia or in El Salvador, children refuse to eat their soup, parents get upset and the family meal is spoiled. Television transforms events into dreams and in their turn, journalists' dreams become reality.

I am bedridden because of a pain that stopped interesting my doctors a while ago. I'm reading a book on the philosophy of history. The carpet is a dark color and the walls are yellowish. The lighting is poor. I know that in the Arab world they have read all the political theories that originated in Germany, the US, or Russia…

Tombs have followed these ideologies, then preceded the new ones, which equally were thrown to the sea. But then why are all these friends and visitors coming to my room, entering my somber Parisian life, the overheated air I breathe, what are they trying to tell me?

In one way or another they come to tell me that they want to go to America! Did we have to live for years under the passage of made-in-Texas Israeli planes, under their perennial harassment, in order to land our dreams next to the crocodiles that swim in the Gulf of Mexico?

During our era's first centuries Syrian craftsmen used to go to Rome to participate in the building of that imperial capital; Caesar was settling our land, and they had to serve him in his own. And today, what are we doing? We are queuing in front of American embassies humbly asking for a visa to the New World: when you die in Beirut you are resurrected in New York.

Those who left many years ago have the one and only fear of losing their green card, that permanent permit of entry into paradise. And I won't dwell on those immigrants who have become such good citizens in their new country that they have changed their names and imagine that the Arabic language sounds like a lamb's bleating.

Bombs flush out the Lebanese with the regularity of a soft tide. People follow the birds flying northwest. Should one submit to either slow or instant death, or rather go and live with those that one has accused of all the world's sins?

But then, if the people of Beirut think about running away from a cursed destiny, who are these other people who keep coming to Beirut, human crickets in spring, storks in winter?

War is the most pleasurable of games. You can get drunk with its smell, its color, its rhythms. You can kill with impunity, be decorated for that. Nations living in peace secretly envy those at war.

After all, that's where the action is. The most odious among the envious are not the readers of newspapers or the moviegoers, no, they are those real voyeurs, the mercenary image-makers, the militiamen of the camera, the vultures of the battlefields, the war correspondents, the televising crews…

Long ago, during a hot summer in Mexico, I was crossing a desiccated gulch near Los Muertos, a dog was lying on the ground in the sun while vultures were performing a beauteous dance before zeroing in on its still-living flesh. Now, from the bellies of huge iron birds all kinds of foreign newsmen disembark in Beirut, clasping their cameras. There is always a breeze to greet them at the airport, even in the middle of summer, when one breathes a mixture of salt water and death, sand and dried bush, the craze for departing and the craze for landing. Time in Beirut is forever hurrying, sucked into the horizon as into a vacuum cleaner. Foreign journalists remain foreign to these matters. They don't know that we vomit in our planes as soon as we enter our country's air space, because of all the contradictions at war within our stomachs. All I can say about the newsmen is that they took interesting views of the Karantina massacre, of Tel Zaatar's siege, of the shelling of Ashrafieh, of the turmoil in Zahleh… They have created the particular aesthetics of the Arab–Mediterranean wars… They have done a bloody good job. In World War II, everything was happening within a grayish zone. In Vietnam the dominant color was green. Here, the sky is blue and blood is red.

Beirut isn't only a privileged laboratory for urban guerrilleros but also a darn good movie lab. Hollywood, Italy, Tokyo cannot compete for realism with the picture taken of an Arab body, still wearing its underwear, that a taxicab filled with passengers was carrying on its roof on its way to the morgue. That made a good close-up with no need for a funeral oration. TV journalists know that they drive the most famous movie directors crazy with envy because they are the authors as well as the actors of an ongoing worldwide performance.

In this room where I am lying and which prevents the branches of the courtyard's linden tree from reaching me, there is a TV set. I am watching the Prince of Wales' marriage. I am waiting in the crowd for his carriage to leave Buckingham Palace. The carriage starts to roll. Charles of England is sitting next to his brother, wearing a navy officer's uniform. Suddenly he looks at the sky, like Prince Andrei in *War and Peace*. He also has, for a moment, the gaze of Lawrence of Arabia, as well as the latter's slightly pink lips.

The prince's retinue, the apparition of the bride carried as a swan on a silver platter, the veil hiding her that will be lifted in Church, everything is fairytale, ravishing. My book on the philosophy of history is put aside. History itself is before me, riding a horse, personified by an authentic prince and princess. But would Charles become king of England? Isn't Mrs. Thatcher the one who exercises real power in his country? Charles becomes therefore a symbol, a drawing on a page. History does not depend on his will. He plays a role. I am watching a play, then. More than a billion spectators are taking part in a game of shadow and light. The simultaneity of this vision watched from every corner of the planet has abolished time's relativity. The clocks are at zero hour.

I sense that the world is ill, like the sun, like myself, degenerating from the beginning, caught in a process of extinction.

Laïla has just arrived from Beirut. She enters my room, dressed in white and wearing her jewelry. I see in her a Mexican deity. Her eyes are shining although they have around them discernible dark circles due to the war; they are prisms through which I can read history's desperate intensity.

"I am on war leave," she tells me. "I have left Beirut for ten days."

"And after?"

"I'm going back. Then I'll try to go to New York. Paris is okay but there's such a feeling of emptiness here. Nowadays even Beirut is better."

"And our West Beirut friends, what are they saying?"

"Oh well! They would go to New York if they

could. Do you imagine them yearning to go to Moscow? The very idea of it kills them with boredom. You know how we Arabs like to be where things are happening. And politically, or for one's safety, it's smarter to be in the US than elsewhere, better to be in the tornado's eye than in its path."

"Tell me, what's new in Beirut besides the shelling?"

"Schlöndorff came to make a movie."

"On Beirut? On the civil war? How is he going to disentangle all the messes we're in. Too many little wars are going on within that single one!"

"No, his movie is not on Beirut. His story is set in Beirut but involves only Germans."

He came for the background, the fury, the chaos and the fires, a sadness that no actor can render, the people's will to live, the burning sea and the poor Arab children who become more beautiful as they get poorer and among whom anyone age seven thinks he is a soccer star. It must be stimulating and inexpensive to film in Beirut. No special effects can compete with the sounds of real war.

"But Schlöndorff did better," says Laila. "He hired the real thing. He found young men from the warring factions and asked them to stage a battle just for his film."

"And they accepted?"

"They were thrilled. Thus the leaders of the different militias, the rightists as well as the leftists, gave orders to stop the real fighting in the center of

Beirut, for a few days, in order to allow their men to reenact a war scene for the German film."

Before the civil war the downtown plaza was Beirut's heart. Buildings of great symbolic value formed its perimeter: a church and a red-light district, the Ministry of Justice and the city's biggest movie theater, jewelry stores and pastry shops. In the heart of that heart there was a monument for the "martyred heroes," the men who at the end of the nineteenth century led an Arab revolt against the Ottoman Empire. Palm trees lined the square.

From that square, one could leave for Asia. One could also say that Asia stopped there, half a mile from the sea. One could have gone from there to Damascus, then Baghdad, then Tehran… Once I boarded the bus for Afghanistan, in the days when I was traveling.

It is on this square that the divorce of a nation took place. Unattended since the war, it has become a garden, enchanted and yet peopled with hostile spirits, the last Mediterranean stronghold of nature. Banana trees have overtaken it, wild grass, crazy vegetation; an orange tree planted itself in its middle, claimed its space, alongside all kinds of reptiles. This downtown plaza is the Middle East's Vietnam. Our indomitable jungle.

There's something of a Chief of Staff in every movie director, there's always authority in a Westerner who happens to be in an Arab land, and something of an actor in any man taking part in a war. This explains why the Lebanese commanders of the militias said "yes" to the German director who turned a red-hot battlefield into a "theater for operations," and I should add that we had all watched too many war movies not to have lost our sanity.

And, you would ask, what was the subject matter of Schlöndorff's movie? A one-sided film, a historical saga, a political indictment? Of course not. It was an adaptation of a novel about a German journalist who had indeed died in Beirut during the bloody events which feed daily the world's news.

On the square mile that constitutes Beirut's center, itself at history's heart, a German journalist had died. For him all images ceased to exist. Another German, a movie director, followed his steps and determined to resurrect him, through an actor, among the places that saw him disappear. The Americans produced *Apocalypse Now* about Vietnam… Schlöndorff would create his own version of the tragic opera that armies stage by their very actions in the midst of ruined landscapes. He chose another war in the Third World, the one in Lebanon.

But does anyone know how to portray war, nowadays, in the cinema, without using sunsets, machine guns, and corpses?

Schlöndorff asked that they manufacture for him two or three dozen corpses in papier-mâché, and these were delivered to him on Saint-Simon Beach, south of Beirut.

"These corpses are so poorly made," said Hassan, one of the extras in the film, a thirteen-year-old who was still a child when he witnessed the Karantina massacre. "I can bring you real ones!" he offered.

Two days later the whole crew was sitting at the Hotel Carlton's hall. It was early afternoon. The Carlton has a view of the sea and the light was reverberating. The hotel is part of the legendary series of hotels in the Arab East where contemporary history was and is still being made: in Damascus, in Cairo, in Palmyra, in Jerusalem, they sheltered the conquerors' dreams and the politicians' betrayals. In Syria, Lawrence slept at the Hotel Baron, General Spears slept at the Beirut Saint-Georges, Allenby at the King David, the Kaiser at the Palmyra Hotel… and Schlöndorff at the Carlton!

The Lebanese youth came in with an enormous burlap bag, emptied it and carefully lined up on the floor, at Schlöndorff's feet and in front of his staff, some fifty skulls and a heap of bones.

"Here they are," he said, "I dug them out these last few days, washed them carefully, and if you want to use them, they're yours. How much will you pay me?"

As it was up to the man in charge to speak, after a silence Schlöndorff asked: "How much do you want?"

"Eight hundred pounds," said the boy.

"No," said Schlöndorff, "it's too much. They're worth five hundred pounds and I won't give a penny more."

"Okay," said the boy, after a longer silence.

annunciation

He walked in slowly and he was stooping, not too much but just a bit, and he said abruptly and in his monotonous tone, don't worry if I'm not walking straight I'm just a whiff tired, no, not too much but I have something to tell you, to ask you, it's maybe not an important thing, but in fact it does matter to me that we discuss this thing together because you know Alissia, and she knows you, you may convince her, I've already told her but she didn't listen, she never does, I never figured out what kind of a world she lives in, now suddenly she's bizarre, not the mom I always had, or thought I had, and it doesn't matter, we're going through a crisis a serious crisis the first huge happening between the two of us since my father died and God bless his soul.

I asked him to sit on my good armchair and he did and I went to make some coffee and he didn't drink his and I drank mine and realized that I had forgotten to put in some sugar, but that's better for everybody's health.

I noticed that his hair had blue-jay tints and that his squinting had gotten worse but there was nothing in his general appearance to worry about and he began by saying, My mother, and quickly after he cleared his throat and a heavy silence fell on us. I didn't urge him to continue, but he did, launching sentences as if they were bubbles and then he pulled his seat closer to mine and I started petting the top of the table then stopped.

This morning I announced it to her, he said, before looking intensely at the floor and after a while he wandered deep into the past and his father returned in his mind and he told me, Since my father's death you know she and I sleep in the same room, you must know, you're such good friends, the one for which Alissia crocheted the curtains in her maiden years as part of her trousseau, grandma must have helped her, who knows, I wasn't born yet, I occupy the empty bed next to hers, these beds are pushed close together because she always feared ghosts angels and demons and I quite often hear her snoring or talking to herself and I never know if she's dreaming or awake, I pretend that I always fall asleep as soon as my ears touch a pillow, any pillow anywhere even on trains and you can see I am still young, so to speak, the stooping is not serious and I told her this morning and she fainted.

Silently, secretly, I was happy that at least he didn't come to review world events with me as they were and still are awfully awful that sometimes it seems that aliens descend from other planets to make all the decisions that mess up our lives and it turned out that I couldn't linger on those thoughts because my visitor went on talking again, telling me, This morning I announced to her the good news that I was going to bring new life to the house and she laid on the floor pale as a lemon and rigid as a plank and I sat down next to her and took her cold hand in mine and after a while I helped her stand on her feet and she looked at me with terror then went down on her knees embracing mine begging me to not utter another sound never do such a terrible thing repeating that I was her only child light of her eyes the product of her belly flesh of her flesh and I agreed that I was all that, that I always have been all that, but now she had to listen because my resolve was in her interest too but she wouldn't stop crying and all she found the energy for was to declare that she will have to ask Father Anastasiou to perform an exorcism upon me and chase the evil spirit out of both my body and my soul.

My mind was distracted as memories concerning my parents' final years were knocking but I dismissed them easily, they had been rehashed too many times and had lost their poignancy over the years. Listening to him became less of a strain as he went on, telling me, I told her she will be good for you she'll wash your clothes, bring you your pills with just the necessary amount of water help you walk down the alley in your old age but she kept refusing to show any sign of life and I panicked I didn't want to have killed my mother a saintly woman beautiful even in her bad days, you must see how she glows under the moonlight on her way back from Vespers and I was saved from hell, I thought at the moment, when she moved her hand and made me believe that she was crying and as everybody knows I can't stand the sight of a woman crying, it breaks my soft heart, I picked up my courage again to explain with a clear voice that I was getting old and had to do something about the future and she rose out of what I had feared to be a coma and sat on the floor and asked for a fan and then threatened to stop eating anymore and let herself die. I hurried to the kitchen and brought a piece of bread with some of her favorite cheese and a glass of raki supposed to bring back one's strength and she pushed her plate away but drank her white liquor and when she asked for more I was saved, as I said, and convinced myself that she was going to agree to what would make me happy.

My visitor went to the bathroom, where he must have washed his face as there were traces of water on his forehead when he returned. He stared at his cup of coffee, which had lost all its luster, all its heat, with utter contempt, and after complaining that it felt too hot in my place he inquired if I had known his mother long before his birth and if she married his father out of convenience or love and did not wait for an answer, being sure that there was none, given that she was barely fifteen when the wedding took place in the village church on the main and only square and probably on the hottest day of that summer. I was, though, one of the children who crowded that wedding. You see, he went on with the flow of his words, these last months I started looking at photographs recently taken of me and they were glaringly showing that I was forty and beyond and they scared me stirred my guts my heart or guts it's all there between my belt and my knees and then I hurried to buy some books not too many just a couple or so and they had pictures oh boy! some pictures like in the movies but better no not better but sadder with the dream taken away they said a lot oh hell were they blunt so explicit that I didn't sleep ever since at least I didn't sleep well and I decided... oh I sure wanted wanted this thing we never mentioned at home all along those insipid years in spite of the nightmare the pain the void and now this morning this very morning and despite the fact that in her despair she yelled and yelled I won't let you go you are my baby my baby my own and if and when you leave this room it will be over my dead body I mean it the sky will come down oh God what have you done to me! I shouted back shouted at her for the first time in my life, Mother, I have to announce to you and I won't take any objection, you have to get it in your head, announce to the world the whole world and that includes my dead father, Mother, I am going to get married!

First Passion

Why is it that when one has more past than future, life's earliest memories acquire a frightful acuity? More and more I realize that my childhood and early adolescence surge in front of me too often, as if they have become a person—a different person each time—who stops me in the street, begs for something I don't understand, and then disappears not behind some corner but into fog, oblivion.

This person could be the self resurrected (or rather returning periodically), asking questions, asking for accountability, demanding the attention it never got back then, yearning eternally for what is yearned for originally and never achieved. We are not only haunted by such ghostly figures but practically hunted, stalked by memories that we don't manage to shake off because something in us knows that their death will be our death. That is, if they ever could die: they may have acquired a life of their own, and there we will never go.

It is true that I was a lonely child, had no brothers or sisters from my mother, my father having had three children from a previous marriage—whom he had abandoned in many ways, and who were living in a different country. There were no little cousins of my own age either. This situation did not make me an especially unhappy girl, but it pushed me, I am sure, to be always seeking friends with whom I could share toys, emotions, thoughts, and games. I was born and raised in Lebanon, amid kids who had extended families—families, it seemed, ad infinitum; I was forever the little outsider whose family appeared extremely meager compared with everyone else's. Even now, friendship always seems to me a bit miraculous and above all, precarious.

Beirut, in my childhood, was a garden city with small neighborhoods, quiet streets, uneventful lives. My school was just a small street away from home; it was run by French nuns who compounded their own Jansenistic brand of Catholicism with a colonial arrogance and gave us a strange kind of education—a bookish one, totally alien to our environment—creating an isolation from both our own traditions and our own inner need for a happy world. In such schools the view of the world was incredibly narrow, dominated by an invisible Father who distributed more punishment than reward to little girls who spoke of sins they couldn't commit and waited for recreation time like inmates in some of the milder prisons of this earth.

Home was a lonely, lovable place. I was aware that my mother was unusually beautiful and that my father was much older; she often made sure this latter fact was known. My emotional life seemed clear: I loved both my parents and that was all.

But that was far from being all. My heart was full of emotions. Emotions about what? I don't think anything was too clear in my childhood. My heart was beating, yes, my mind was busy, swimming in the sea was such a happy experience, day after day in the summer, when nuns weren't around for a change.

Playing with classmates was the highest emotional reward: running in the school's courtyard, chatting endlessly on the way home around four o'clock, dragging my feet, chewing time, arriving thirty minutes later than expected. I was usually trying to be the focus of attention, and most of the time I was. As children must select a best friend, I paired off mostly with a little classmate my age, Anissa Chaker. I remember her face, her appearance, as if I saw her only a few weeks ago. She had green-blue eyes, very curly black hair, rather pale skin, and high cheekbones. She lived a few blocks down the road, halfway between the seashore and my house. Her mother had died, and she lived with her father and three older brothers. My mother liked her; I think she felt reassured that she came from a "good family." So I was regularly—and I would say solemnly— "sent" to play with Anissa in her beautiful, traditional house, which was built of stone, with arches and a balcony. This started when I was, I think, seven and went on for a few years. (In fact, I remained a friend of Anissa's till late adolescence, until the younger of her brothers fell in love with me and became an insistent boyfriend, taking me to horse races and to watch a stranger game called pigeon hunting, where he would bet on the guy who would bring down a pigeon with a single shot. Little by little I lost track of him, and then of her, after I went to finish college in Paris.)

In our classrooms the children were seated on benches, each with two desks that opened vertically and in which we could leave our books and note-books. An ink pot was inserted on the right side of the case. We were assigned our seats by the teacher nun. It happened—I must have been age nine—that I was seated next to a girl whose name was Helen. I liked Helen the very first day we sat next to each other. She was quiet, noticeably quiet. I was a restless child and rather outgoing, proud of stirring things up, admired by the teachers for my studies and dreaded by them for my lack of discipline.

I don't think it took me long before I realized that Helen was unlike all the other kids. Gradually I grew to feel that there was a difference in my eyes (or rather I should say my heart) between Anissa and Helen. Anissa remained my friend, with all the comfortable feelings that friendship produces, all the freedom that it entails. I could run with her in the schoolyard, eat cake at her home, chat, laugh, spend hours in her garden. But with Helen, for the first time in my life I felt shy, intimidated, awkward in front of another child, and I was aware of it and couldn't manage the situation. I was too serious with her, too attentive, exceedingly proud to walk with her until we reached her street, happy for the privilege of being invited into her home, where she had an older sister and an older brother. Anything concerning her seemed of the utmost importance and glamour. Why was her home big and rather sad, silent, formal? It impressed me to no end.

This went on for two years. I "loved" Helen differently from anybody else, almost as in the movies, not quite, though not unlike, either. Because of her I entered that zone that one experiences in youth, of half-denials, half-truths about oneself and one's affections, and I remained there for quite a while—until my mid-twenties, and through several other passions. It is a tragic situation, due to this sixth sense that we have for what is expected from us and what is not, what is allowed and what is considered shameful. Why and how we have it, I don't really know, but it happens early in life, and with some people never gets resolved.

I discovered within my heart a kind of secret space that Helen inhabited, where I would talk to her, and where I would notice her extreme beauty—which was real, not merely imagined. She had the most beautiful eyes I ever saw in my whole life, and later I realized that they looked like Garbo's—she always looked a bit sleepy when she looked at me (and at anything). Her eyes were not blue but the color of dark honey, and they looked clearer when the sun hit them; her eyelashes made huge shadows on them, practically down to her cheeks. I was speechless most of the time with her, thinking of her while she was present, exactly as I would feel ten or twelve years later when I fell in love—I wouldn't say more deeply, but more explicitly and more violently—with a woman I met in Paris during my student years.

Beirut in the thirties was itself a preadolescent city: newly installed as a capital for a nation carved out by the Allies from Syria. It smelled of jasmine and orange blossoms, and you could look at the sea from almost any street. I already loved it as a child, sensed its beauty and enjoyed any contact with it, such as going to the market with my father or running down the street to the swimming places. The most mysterious of all experiences, back then, was seeing a movie. Oh, the movies, what a love affair, what a passion for the unreachable! There were few cinemas in the city and children were not supposed to be taken to them, but my mother had (as I understood later) a boyfriend, and she would go to the cinema with him and take me along, usually in the evening and in the winter. I would fill my head with the black-and-white shimmering of the screen and see good-looking grown-ups come very close to each other to create a languorous atmosphere that I called love. Early on movies formed my sensibilities (for better or worse), and movie stars became my archetypes of desirability. Men and women were equally desirable, equally magical, with maybe Garbo having an edge on them all.

In the schoolyard I would tell the kids assembled around me of the things I saw. One day I was caught by a wretched nun in the middle of a dance performance—I think Garbo's mazurka—that I was giving as a means of explanation. I was deprived of recreation for two weeks, but all this just increased my fascination for the erotic quality of black-and-white moving images, to such a point that many decades later I still find something of that undying quality in even such benign images as Ansel Adams's flowers or trees.

What made things even more magical was that a new cinema, with velvety red seats and huge red curtains, had just opened, the most beautiful, the most prestigious in the city, and that cinema, the Roxy, belonged to little Helen's uncle! So from the time I was not yet eleven until much later, even when I didn't see Helen anymore, the Roxy was tied to her image. The visits to the Roxy were enhanced by the fact that that uncle was rumored to have lived in America (something only connected to movies) and had come back to add to the city its newest dream house. That was the place where through the years I watched *Blood and Sand*, *The Scarlet Empress*, *Anna Karenina*, and, later, *The Barefoot Contessa*. And on and on… Given the shyness (or the awe)

Helen created in me, she was barely closer than the movie stars, all too present in my head and in my heart, and so little or not at all in my everyday world.

Something happened, I can't remember what, but I was mad at her for something—or nothing, that's the whole point—and stopped talking to her although we still sat on the same bench. I felt a mixture of sorrow and some other feeling I couldn't define, even then, and I retreated into myself when it came to her—I could not get out of that mood that had taken hold of me. My sadness must have been so evident that one of our teachers, a young lay teacher, who must have seen how much we were friends, came to me one afternoon just when class had ended and stopped Helen on her way out. She brought us together saying, "Come on, little ones, you have to make up." And looking at me she said, "I know how fond of her you are, so let's stop this nonsense." I remember that I had been desperately waiting for such a moment, but—and I wish I knew for sure why, because that situation recreated itself later with other people, and I always reacted the same way and lived to regret it—I refused to open up and admit that things weren't normal, that the little storm, certainly all of my own doing, had gone away. Thus I went on playing with all the children save the one I was desperately missing.

We must have been then in the second year of our relationship, somewhere between friendship and something else we were too young to name, yet we were aware of its intensity, of the trouble, the stirrings it was creating in our souls. I attribute those feelings to Helen as well because by then she wasn't talking much to anybody but me, and with me she was quiet, aloof, dreamy, or just content. After the scene of the impossible reconciliation (which I still regret), she went her solitary way, but not for long. She became friends with an interesting schoolmate whom I knew a bit, a red-haired and blue-eyed Russian girl who was, I learned later, the daughter of an exiled Azerbaijani prince who was living in Moscow when the Revolution erupted and who had sought refuge in Lebanon. Tania Nahidchevansky was her name. I was intrigued by both the person and the name, and when Helen and she became "best friends," I would look at them and think how lucky Tania was and that I would never reestablish the exclusivity I had once had with Helen.

(I think that Tania and I did talk to each other, the more so because Tania was an outgoing child, aware of her influence on others, of her special presence and her exotic appeal in our little crowd.)

Around age eleven the children in that French system of education had to pass an exam, a "certificate" signaling the end of elementary school. The nuns built a lot of expectation around that end-of-the-year examination, especially because failure meant one could be prevented from going on to the next level of classes. We needed a card for that, with a picture glued on it, the equivalent of a passport photo. There were about twenty of us in that class, and we all went to the photographer, and I think I talked to Helen then. We were each given two or three more pictures than needed, and we began to exchange them with our friends, and Helen gave me her picture and I gave her mine.

In my house I didn't have much that was exclusively mine, but I had a little drawer where I kept my pencils, erasers, pencil sharpener, and maybe a few notebooks. I put Helen's picture in a corner, on top of the other things, and every time I opened the drawer I would look at it, bring it close to my face, and once in a while kiss it, barely, and put it away again. One day I put a little flower on it, which left some pollen, a tiny yellow spot, and I was so relieved to see that it didn't harm her face but was close to the corner of the picture.

My own wanderings, my nomadic university life, my incapacity to transfer many belongings from place to place, and ultimately the war in Lebanon, which followed my settling in California—all that forced me to discard a lot in my life and end up with very few documents from the past. Even the most valuable ones were lost, but that little picture of Helen appears once in a while when I reshuffle some of my old papers.

Helen also told me that she was changing schools, that Tania was doing the same, and that they were going to the Collège Protestant Français, the only non-Catholic French school in the city. It was more expensive than the Catholic ones and had a prestige of its own, as it was run by Mademoiselle Weigman, a strong-headed woman who is now quite famous. Her students were some of the richest, most beautiful, and most intelligent girls. Something was unique about the school, and in Catholic circles it was always rumored that it wasn't religiously correct to go there. I came home and told my mother that I wanted to change schools too. Her reaction was immediate: "They don't believe in God there!" Although she was Greek, born in Smyrna and exiled in Beirut, she must have heard such slander and believed it. There was no chance that I would go to that school.

I knew that Helen's company was lost to me. I thought about it constantly, in that realm of our minds where some ideas, ideas that are also feelings, linger in a permanent though weightless way; it is a melancholic cloud, a thin veil, which becomes all too familiar and takes years to disappear, if it ever does.

A year or so later—I must have been twelve or thirteen—I was bicycling on the Corniche, the wonderful avenue that borders the sea and which was walking distance from my home. Somehow my mother had allowed me to learn to ride a bicycle, and there was in the neighborhood a little store where for a few piasters one could rent one of those graceful little machines. Very few people rented them for pleasure, and they were mostly young boys. But one afternoon my path crossed Helen's and Tania's;

they too were bicycling on the Corniche, and they waved at me. I was so surprised to see them that I was almost run over by a passing car; I swerved and fell. The car stopped, the driver made sure that I was all right, and when I stood and got back on the bike the two girls were already far away. I rode in the opposite direction, returned my bicycle, and went home.

Time passed, including World War II, my early university years, and studies in Paris, Berkeley, and Harvard. I settled in California, which I love and still call home, but sometime before the beginning of the Lebanese civil war I had returned briefly to Beirut (only to be forced by the fighting to come back to the United States). In Beirut there was a well-known little café called The Horseshoe, popular among the artists of the city and some journalists. Next to it, I discovered that a store selling luxurious clothes had opened during my prolonged absence. It belonged to Helen's sister, Mary, and I was moved to have fallen upon traces of Helen. (Mary had an American name because the family emigrated to the States and it was only after the children were born that they returned to Lebanon. That explained why there was something special about those two little girls who had gone to school with me.)

One day, seeing Helen through the front window, I entered the store and said hello to my old friend. She didn't show much surprise, but a faint smile and a passing light in her perpetually beautiful eyes encouraged me to say a few words. I learned that she was married and had two children. That was almost all she had to say. "What are you doing now?" I asked.

It was summertime, and she said that she was going to the beach. "Why don't you come with me?" she said, and I thought I would. But I didn't. I noticed that she was as pale as when she was little, as diffident, as dreamlike. If I had just met her for the first time, I would have found her lovable, appealing, the type of person I would have liked to know, in her quiet way. It was as if the separation never existed, as if we were the children we had been: shy, innocent, with a whole imprecise space ahead of us, with no worries, no knowledge of any kind, no past and no notion of future, two little beings happy to be together and not even aware of that happiness.

But I didn't go to the beach. I don't even want to know if I was right or wrong. In the course of my life I have thought about love over and over again, and I still do: Love is the most important matter we have to deal with, but it is always the hardest. It comes about like a wave of infinite strength and creates the fear of drowning; it inhibits our intelligence, paralyzes our will, looks hopeless from the start. At least this is how it must appear to most people, and how I have always experienced it. It bypasses the channels of reason; it is foolish by essence and seems to spring from some inner region of the mind—or of the soul—where panic resides. It creates a desperate need, the need to arrest in space and time the person beloved; it has to do with the absolute. It usually ends in tragedy because it is in essence a fever, a flame, an energy that moves with no control and brings aberration to our behavior. This is why everyone kills his or her own love, out of desperation: we lose the battle in fearing to lose it, we prefer to die than to doubt, we suffer in order not to suffer; we are doomed, and we are wrong.

My Friend Kate

When I first saw her there was a sense of deep melancholy about her, which could have been worrisome, but there was also an elegance that impressed me, and it turned out that we became friends pretty soon after.

America was then very foreign to me, everything she said or did was of great interest: through her I was initiated to all the little and apparently insignificant things that make a new world. We were in the Bay Area but when we met she had just arrived from Ohio, and that entrenched her solidly in the heart of the land and I was thrilled to know somebody so rooted in the country.

One day she introduced me to her friend Dean, a good-looking fellow who had been her childhood neighbor and knew her whole family. Little by little I discovered that she was quite in love with him, in a different way, for it didn't take much time for her to let me know that Dean was gay and living in San

Francisco with a young man who was originally from Oklahoma. Tony was his name, and Tony was known for his infatuation with trains.

In those days—the beginning of the sixties—I was working for a design firm, as I had a degree from an art institute in Paris. Kate (that's her name) was the librarian of one of Marin County's public libraries. She had a beautiful car and was happy to be in California, although, I learned later, she had come to San Francisco on a sudden urge prompted by one of Dean's phone calls. She had secured a retirement place for her mother and driven West only to be told by him that he was on his way to New York… That's about the time I met her, when there was something tragic about her, and she told me over a few drinks in the shine and sounds of the Jazz Workshop that after Dean had gone, she had driven to the Golden Gate with the purpose of jumping off the bridge. "I didn't," she said, "it was too awful."

For years, I could say for a few decades, Kate remained my best friend. At its start our friendship had a lot to do with the fact that I was much younger and she represented a kind of archetypal American in my eyes. One has to know that for some foreigners their encounter with America is a phenomenon of great magnitude. She was extremely thin, a very determined person, the quintessential image of a Yankee. We did many things together, trips to the Monterey Jazz Festival, weekends on the Mendocino

Coast. Little by little our conversations were opening up my mind to an America I didn't know.

She was born in Warren, Ohio, to a father who was Pennsylvania Dutch, a businessman who lost everything in the Great Depression. "He lost his mind too," she used to add to her story. On her mother's side, Kate was English, although her mother's grandma was French. Kate's grandmother was a DAR and she explained to me what the "D," "A," and "R" stood for. "Of course," added Kate, repeating the story many times, "I could prove that she was also Mayflower. But I never took the time. What's the use…?"

The family photographs that she showed me quite a few times were brownish, and she was always surrounded by older people, being an only child and with no cousins on either side. To be an American so rooted in the history of the country and so alone! I often wondered.

After the Depression, when Kate in her early twenties had lost half a million shares in copper mines, in addition to what her mother had lost, and after her father died within a few years, something had to be done to keep the mother and the mother's unmarried sister alive: Kate worked on an itinerant library that toured a series of small towns all around Warren. That's how she became an on-the-job trained librarian and the breadwinner for the three of them. Dean was her younger neighbor, and she became one night, and only for that night, his first and only woman. Neither forgot that experience and they remained attached to each other for the rest of their lives.

I loved all the stories about Kate's early life. They used to take place in my imagination, in some round and deep landscape with blurred trees, in fact blurred seasons, in a time that was itself imprecise, a Midwestern "somewhere," a mythical time, to be honest, a wonderful construct of our two minds.

There was magic to these days that were unfolding in front of me. From Warren we used to move to Columbus, the capital of state, I thought, and to Cleveland, and sometimes I didn't know exactly where we were, but it was Ohio, for sure, and then I learned the names of the best pitchers, one of them having lived on Euclid Avenue when Kate had moved to Cleveland.

Cleveland itself was a magic name, and Kate had two loves, Dean and Margaret. Margaret was a childhood friend, recurring in our conversations. She was related to the Clevelands, founders of the city. Her grandfather's farm had the prestige of having been the land on which, later, the Cleveland Museum of Modern Art would be built. As that museum has one of the most beautiful Monets that I ever saw, Margaret acquired in my eyes a special aura. This was not reciprocated, though; I remained for her an intruder who might as well have come from another planet. When she came to visit in California, and I was also invited to lunch, I would follow, without interfering, recollections of which both she and Kate were particularly fond: how, for example, John D. Rockefeller went to the same Baptist church as Kate's father, and how her father would come home at the end of the service and say that the price of oil must have gone up because John D. had added a dime to the Sunday collection. They also talked about the Packard boys, the ones who built the cars I used to see in movies, boys who made a lot of noise cruising the main street of Warren! That's what Kate used to repeat quite often, oh yes, she also mentioned the Tafts, and Margaret's only child grew to go to college with one of the Tafts' boys, and as he was Kate's god-child I met him quite often, when he was visiting her on his way to the ski slopes of Tahoe.

But Margaret lived in Danbury, somewhere in Connecticut, and that gave Kate many occasions for declaring that she herself wasn't an Easterner any-more, but a Californian, which was true enough, given that she had traded vodka for California Chenin blanc and Mayacamas reds.

One day when I asked if Ohio was Eastern or part of the Midwest, they both said simultaneously that it was both things and they added, together again, that it was once a western frontier and, of course, Margaret's great-grandfathers had been the heroes of that migration… That's also when I heard about Angie, Kate's maternal grandma: Angie was "quite a character," not an Ohioan by birth, and famous as a charter member of the Prohibition Party.

Angie even moved her family to Prohibition Park, near Boston. I think I even heard that she was on speaking terms with both angels and demons, knowing very well what they were up to: she knew demons helped some otherwise good citizens fill their bathtubs with homemade alcohol—no, Kate assured me, that did not happen in Prohibition Park.

I also discovered that there was something religious in Kate, even if she represented the most thorough agnosticism that I ever encountered. A French woman living in Tiburon had told me that Kate reminded her of some eighteenth-century marquise, of Voltaire and Diderot, because of her elegance and skepticism, and the generosity of her spirit in spite of her total lack of illusions. But, nonetheless, there was something utterly religious about the absolute value that she put on her own dignity, a way that for her resolved the question of God.

There was a bond between Dean, Margaret, and Kate, which appeared to be unbreakable, almost ancient. But Dean, during one of his stays in New York, used Kate's credit with a fashionable store, and bought two pairs of pants for himself… Kate mentioned it to Margaret, who became furious: how could anyone take advantage of a woman with a salary as small as Kate's? That year Dean did not get a Christmas card from Margaret, and never after.

Kate was sorry. Deeply so. The more so because Dean was, according to her own expression, "deteriorating": he was losing his friends, having borrowed money from almost every one, and was losing his jobs: during World War II he had been an intelligence officer in the British Army (yes!), and had met Durrell somewhere in Egypt, and after that it was "downhill." He ended up teaching high school in San Francisco, and couldn't stand it, he dreamed of writing a novel, of sending a story to the *New Yorker*, his favorite magazine. He was employed as a postman, but he was chatting too much with old ladies waiting at the mailbox, and got fired. He managed to land a job as a gardener around Haight-Ashbury, but by then he had become an alcoholic and Kate had to count the many empty bottles hidden under his bed. It's true that Tony had left him, like that, suddenly, without a trace. Kate was worried because Dean was also a diabetic and one evening, as she and I were eating hamburgers at Marin Joe's and I was pouring plenty of ketchup on my plate, she looked worried and told me: "You know, Margaret, Dean, and I, back in Ohio, just after the Depression, we swore one day—a winter day and in front of the fireplace—that we were going to be together at the end of the century, at the beginning of the new millennium. I want to see that millennium start, that January the first of the year 2000, and I know we'll make it." She looked calm, and there were so many repressed dreams in her eyes that I was sure that this one was going to be fulfilled. She reminded me of a lake forever calm, forever flowing.

Dean was fired from his gardening job and went on unemployment. His phone calls were becoming lengthy and his stories repetitive. Kate would say: "He isn't fun anymore." There was more to it than that casual remark. She herself became edgy, visiting him more often, while dreading the visits. One late evening, when California was drenched in one of its apocalyptic storms, she insisted on going to the city. That night I was awakened by her physician, who told me over the phone that Kate had been found in her car, off the highway, in Marin, just after the tunnel. Nobody figured out what really happened. Kate didn't remember a thing, only that she found herself on a hospital bed. The car was squeezed like an accordion and her slender frame was covered with bruises. Her face was swollen and her eyes barely visible. When I went to visit her, the first thing she said was: "You see. I told you I'm going to live to be 94, at least!"

The ebullient sixties were over. Life was settling down and people were counting their blessings and their losses. At the public libraries, the readers were gradually asking for new kinds of books. Something had turned sour. I was getting restless, again, as I do every few years, and I left the Bay Area and went to Europe.

When I returned to Marin County it was, at least for me, a new America. Some spirit of seriousness had taken hold of the minds of those I knew. The numbers of pleasure boats all over the Bay had increased, but the winds, somehow, were tame.

Kate wasn't driving to the city much anymore. Her bridge club and some new friends she'd made were taking all her time and attention. Whenever I asked about Dean, the answer would be, "How do you want him to be? He brought it all on himself." Yes, Dean was hospitalized in the middle of February, he had pneumonia and other complications, and his nurse asked Kate to come and see him, and she refused, and he died a few days after his final request. Kate was pale and determined not to utter a single word about the event. And ever since she wouldn't say a word about him.

I settled in San Francisco, happy to have found both a new job and a new apartment, this one with a view of the water. The city lifted my spirit. I wanted to recapture something of my early days in California, wanted to feel again as though I were at the edge of the world, with my back turned to the past, both its joys and failures. I was looking for a feeling of daring transience and I found it.

Kate was barely managing with her very small income. Ever since the Depression she had learned to live with very little without having to admit poverty. She watched baseball games, even doubleheaders. She got excited about golf and her nightly glass of white wine. She gave up smoking and sold her two-door BMW. She even found a studio in a complex for senior citizens: she hated the word and even the place, in the beginning, but she managed to befriend the gardener and she repeated to him regularly a few stories about her parents' garden in Warren (it had begonias and squirrels) and the trains she rode on the lap of her maternal uncle Holloway. The gardener tried to teach her some special flower names but she rebelled: besides jazz, she loved only Gertrude's books and Shakespeare.

Everything seemed fine and she appeared to be cruising pretty well the tedious waves of the passing years until very recently, when the only witness to the 89 years of her life, her friend Margaret, on a hot afternoon by the Chesapeake Bay, where her son had moved her, passed away. Her son, John, had to give Kate the terrible news by telephone. He didn't know how to go about it and just said: "Mother has died. This morning mother has died." As she could hardly hear, and sensing trouble, she asked: "Whose mother, what mother?" and he answered: "Margaret. Our Margaret. She is no more."

I said to wait a minute, that I was coming, and I did hurry and found her sitting in her armchair in front of a silent TV, her door as usual unlocked. Her studio was gray and beige and the clock was ticking. "How are you?" I said, and she said: "All right." She did not repeat the news to me. She looked awfully frail and was wobbly when she tried to stand and bring me something from the kitchen. "Oh! Please sit," I begged, and her brown eyes, which had kept their look of longing for a lifetime, gazed at my face, and beyond, and I said that I was sorry, but she remained silent. She saw my tears coming down my cheeks and I saw her shake and she tried to reassure me: "Don't cry," she spoke softly, "we'll make it. I don't understand why Margaret quit. There are only four years left. I guess that for hers and Dean's sake, as much as for my own, I will face the turn of the millennium all by myself… unless you join me there, too."

Eavesdropping

At the corner of Rue du Parc Royal and Rue de Turenne there's a fine restaurant where I go whenever I happen to be in that arrondissement around lunch hour. Today I made a tour of some art galleries with my friend Simone. A cold day with Christmas looming at the end of the week, a wonderful combination of events for being carefree and rediscovering Paris.

We entered the Café des Musées and chose a corner near a window that has just two tables set side by side and a hook on the wall for hanging coats. The place was busy and the waitress not as prompt as usual, but it didn't matter. When at last she arrived with the menus, we ordered a *soupe de cresson*, a pumpkin soup, beef and fish. A bottle of wine.

A young couple arrived and sat at the next table. A feeling of friendly curiosity took hold of us. The rest of the café could have meandered and gone to wherever it wanted, we were happily and safely tucked between a view of the street, nice momentary neighbors and the back of the bar.

At my left was a youngish woman wearing a black sweater and blue jeans. Facing her was a man, young but already a bit plump. I found him loveable.

He told her—and that was the first sentence he uttered—"Let's have a glass of champagne." She said: "No," and it was clear that she meant it. A little while later, with a soft voice, he added: "But it's Christmas."

The waitress, making her rounds, came, left, and returned. They ordered beef stew with carrots and potatoes. Same menu for both. He settled for a quart of house wine. She hurried to object: "You should not drink at noon, it makes one feel groggy, heavy."

Shaking his head, speaking in a neutral tone of voice, and with a gesture of his right hand as though waving goodbye to a friend, he ordered a big bottle of Evian water.

I took a quick look at her and saw a stern face and tight lips: she's already getting old, I thought. I took his side, looking for more reasons to like him. He didn't wear a black sweater but a nice brown shirt under a soft corduroy jacket that made me remember a similar one I wore in my student days in the same city. I noticed that his pupils were greenish with darker circles around them. He was a benevolent fellow, I decided. He was obviously begging for a smile, for a sign, an intimation of some complicity between them, but nothing was coming from her eyes besides a blank look.

When the plates arrived and she started to eat, she seemed to relax. I told my friend Simone, in a language that I was sure neither of them would understand, that while the woman was pushing a lot of bread in her mouth, the guy was looking so gentlemanly.

I was enjoying my fish and vegetables and noticed that our bottle of wine was already empty. We were chatting when Simone, out of the blue, made the remark that, although she liked the neighborhood we were in, she hated the number 96 bus.

"Why?" I asked.

"It's always crowded."

"It depends on the hour."

"No, it's always crowded and it stinks."

"Oh," I said, "it's a nice day. The season has been unusually mild. Funny."

"Yes, but we didn't go on a vacation. All our friends have."

Suddenly, the woman next to me raised her voice:

"What's this business of feeling sorry for your mother?! She's fine in her house in Normandy. She likes it. There's no problem."

"But she's all alone. And at Christmas…"

"She believes in nothing. Not in religion, and certainly not in you."

"She lost her husband, my father, that's been tough on her."

"Not tougher than having cancer."

"Why are you bringing up cancer? What does it have to do with anything?"

He took his eyeglasses off and wiped them. He carefully put them back on his nose. He was looking for something to say that would calm her down. He moved his lips imperceptibly. He lost interest in his food, pushed his plate slightly away from him.

She finished her meal and snatched his piece of bread and dipped it in his plate and ate all the sauce.

We brought up the question of wanting to move one day, the apartment being too dark in winter.

"I need to see trees from the windows," I said

"So do I," said Simone. "I need more space, a lot of space. I can't think where we are. When the holidays are over I will start looking."

"This time, I hope we do it."

It was our turn for dessert. After much discussion we agreed on pears marinated in wine. The pears were small but tasty and the wine mixed with the cream. My friend said seriously:

"The hot wine we had in the brasserie the other day was better."

"Which hot wine, this is cold wine!"

My attention moved back to the table next to us. Now the young man was talking about his job. I understood that he was not fond of his boss, but when she asked him why he was always bringing the matter up while doing nothing about his situation he routinely replied that after all his salary was pretty good compared to what his friends were earning elsewhere with jobs more or less similar.

I sensed that underneath it all he was wanting to bring his face nearer to hers, bending over, smiling, caressing her with his eyes, covering her with an air of happy expectation.

The waitress came and took their dishes away. She returned with the list of the desserts and the woman let her know that she would skip dessert and have just a cup of coffee. Then the waitress turned to him. He spontaneously, joyfully ordered a baba-au-rhum. The woman blew up.

The baba-au-rhum innocently arrived and stared her in the face. She was biting her nails and closing her fists. I could hear her breathe. When he started to bring a bite from the baba to his mouth she sprung and stopped his arm in mid-air while it was holding the spoon.

"You will smell like alcohol," she said.

"It doesn't matter," I heard him say, "we're going to my place." He freed his arm and took her hands in his. "We're going to my place," he insisted, and he dared whisper: "I love you… and it's Christmas."

She dismissed his supplication. She warned him that he was on his way to becoming an alcoholic, that he was already one, that she was useless to him because he never listened to her, she was wasting her time… and that was that.

She stood up, threw the white napkin on the floor, picked up her coat from the hook and left. He looked in the direction of the door. His whole body was saying that he wanted to follow her, try to bring her to reason, wanted badly to sleep with her in his warm and tidy studio apartment, but he was confused, or rather wounded. He couldn't leave immediately, he had to wait and pay the bill. He was standing, embarrassed, and when the waitress finally came she behaved as if she hadn't noticed that he hadn't touched his baba. He paid. He swiftly wiped a tear and then, like a worn-out toy, he just sat back on his chair.

As for me, I felt like staying a bit more but there was no reason to. The lunch was over. For the first time in many years I dreaded to climb on the 96.

Yellow, Yellow Cab

We drank wine around a checkered tablecloth, sitting in a restaurant in the East Village, not far from my hotel. We hadn't been in touch for quite a while. When I asked what she was doing lately I didn't expect her answer. She replied that she had decided to become a taxi driver.

Skippy can be an extremely tense person. Her mixture of boldness and shyness creates an instability that often discourages any serous communication. Most of her friends have drifted away from her, not necessarily because she did anything wrong but because they were themselves restless addicts, confused about their lives or running away from some inner terror that pushed them unexpectedly onto highways, trains, and buses, and, for the richer ones, international travels.

Her father was a trapper. She never got a chance to know him well, as he disappeared in a snowstorm when she was only five years old. Her mother then married a Filipino worker who had come one day to fix the bathtub and some deficient appliances. When asked about her childhood she would invariably counter-ask: "Should I have had any childhood?"

I was surprised that she had given up her former job, and as I hadn't seen or heard from her for a couple of years, there was much to catch up on. When our lunch was over she offered to give me a ride to wherever I wanted. We were in a joyous mood. "Let's have a tour of Brooklyn," I proposed. She agreed.

Crossing the Brooklyn Bridge is always exhilarating. We drove through the streets. I wanted to go near the ocean but somehow we found ourselves at a spot where, I have to admit, the view of Manhattan was incredibly beautiful. We parked and stayed in the car; that's the best place to chat, I've always felt. Moving from one subject to another I learned that, just a few months before, she had undergone a treatment for drug addiction. "It was tough going," she said, "with all those addicts. Now, I won't even have more than one or two glasses of wine although, I swear, I was never an alcoholic." She added that being a taxi driver was what she needed. "Pretty anonymous. And I love driving at night. The whole city is different then. It's mine. I love it." When I inquired how long she thought she would keep at it, she smiled and said: "I don't want to know."

I asked her if she ever ran into trouble in her new job. She laughed. She explained that when she suspected from afar that somebody meant danger she would put her flag up, pretending that she was on her way home. "That's a good trick," she said. She looked determined. Nobody was ever going to tell her what to do. Nobody was ever going to break the first line of her defenses. Her solitude was her pride. In the privacy of my own memory I recollected how she once gave up her relation with a woman she loved just to prove to her that she didn't need her, that she had never cared for her, and it was all because of a compulsive need to hurt, to prove to herself that she could hurt—that she was totally "free."

Suddenly, she confided: "People are different at night. Looser. Readier for the unexpected. They seem to feel safe with a woman driver. They're sometimes eager to talk. Of course, it's monologues that I hear, little engines that keep going, ribbons of words that pour out from their mouths and get lost in the air like tobacco smoke. I don't mind. I have my own thoughts."

༄

It was in the *New York Times*: "Ex-top executive murdered by a prostitute." Just in time for the morning edition, ahead of the tabloids.

I wondered: what's the world coming to? But then I felt a strange itch, as if ants were moving up my spine, my hands freezing. I went on reading. I was numb.

It was indeed written that Fancy Lee, a "famous" prostitute well known by the police department, was arrested under the suspicion that she had murdered Frances Lewis, former CEO of the Flying Instruments Company. The reporter didn't insist on the fact that the victim was now a cab driver, probably because he didn't yet know much about her latest profession.

A rush of thoughts and emotions invaded my mind. I loved Skippy the way one loves a flower, or a window on a particularly beautiful view. She was refreshingly intelligent, with the kind of naïveté that often comes with that. Sometimes I told myself that if America had been run by her likes we wouldn't have been in the mess we are now. That's silly thinking, yes, but it was a tribute to her integrity.

After many phone calls and some pulling of strings I managed, a while later, to visit Fancy Lee in the city jail.

The woman I met was full of anger, though obviously sad and worried. I don't know what she had been told about my visit's purpose, but she showed no reluctance to talk. The story had been rehashed by the papers and by now she was so worn out that it made no difference to her to whom she was speaking and why.

When I assured her that I was not one more journalist who'd come to harass her, she relaxed, and sensing that I was not unfriendly, she laid out the sequence of the fatal events:

"It was a bad night. There were bad vibes all over. The last client who took me up to his room down Second Avenue was a mess of a guy. Messy and messed up. He threw up his dinner before laying me down. All along I was praying: O God, make him come quick! I'm a Catholic, if you care to know, but that doesn't make it easier. It's a business some of us end up doing. No sentiments, no weirdness, a transaction like in any other trade. With the difference that we have to look calm, appealing, even willing, although we smell danger at every corner we stand on. The entrance to the hotel was painted green, bathtub green. He was green too. Sick, body and soul. When I asked him to pay me so I could leave, he laid flat on his face. His mouth was foaming. I went into his pocket and found a single ten-dollar bill only, and took it. Nothing would have kept me one second longer in that room, that animal's lair.

"Outside, it was snowing much harder than when we went in. A real tempest had unleashed itself on the street. I stopped the cab, surprised to find a woman driving the damn thing in such weather and at such an hour. I said, Brooklyn? And she said no, said that she was going to make a right turn and go uptown, go home. It's true that she didn't have her light on and I shouldn't have signaled her to stop, but I did, and after she had refused, she changed her mind.

"I killed nobody. I defended myself. In my profession, you have to act soft and be hard. It's like being in a boxing ring, only it doesn't seem like it. We're in a game for survival. We wear shiny underwear but our skin is tough. My body is sheer iron. It's rusting alright, but it has to stay tough. You women with bank accounts and fancy husbands will never imagine what we have to go through, day after day, night after night, and stop telling us that it's all a matter of choice… It's a whole underworld parallel to yours, and so different, good God, so different. She followed me to my flat, parked the car, yes, in front of my door. It was freezing cold, beastly cold. She asked to come up and rest a bit and the stupid me got soft for a change, and it taught me a lesson, a lesson I won't forget if I ever come out alive from this ordeal.

"Before reaching my place she lost her way and in these early hours that are neither dark nor lit we found ourselves wandering through the most wretched neighborhoods of Brooklyn where erratic shadows were mixing with the falling sheets of snow. The counter was clicking and I was getting upset, thinking that she was doing it on purpose, trying to gouge money out of me, but she seemed to guess my thoughts and she stopped the machine and made it clear that she wasn't going to charge me for her confusion.

"At one point I decided that she must have been a loony. She asked if the black people were having a rough time in Brooklyn. Black or white, they're all the same. One day you get a guy threatening you with a knife, the next another who tries to break your jaw because you won't kiss him, and that's when they don't hire you just to wet you all over with their tears, because their mothers were cruel to them, so they always say."

Was she avoiding telling what really happened that night? I wondered. I did pose the question quite bluntly. She went on with the story as if I hadn't interrupted her.

"Something in me made me feel sorry for her. I gave her some cognac, she refused to drink it at first, and then suddenly she gulped it down. There was panic in her eyes. I expected her to leave soon after, but when she saw me go toward the door she made a pass at me, becoming amorous or whatever, and I was so tired, and disgusted. It's bad enough to have men always wanting to jump me, but a woman! I didn't need that. I turned rude, yes, I had to. And when she pretended that she wouldn't hurt a fly, that she meant no harm, that I was beautiful and that we both were lonely people, when she poured out all this nonsense, it blew my top! Me, beautiful, even men don't tell me such things anymore... and lonely? Wherever I am it's always crowded, too crowded for my own good! I don't have the luxury of feeling lonely, she should have known that. But no, she was too weird for my straight business. In my own way, I'm an honest woman. She abused my hospitality, there, with me being exhausted, half-asleep, and was I flabbergasted when I learned later that she had been a big shot in a big firm!

"How would I have imagined such a thing—all I met was a woman driver behaving like a drunken sailor in the wee hours of the night. She became sort of desperate and aggressive. She clung onto me with all her weight, threatened and cursed, and the situation became scary, violent, chaotic, insane. I instinctively reacted, used my karate skills—to survive in the street you have to learn such tricks—and I used them so lightly, more to scare her off than hurt her for real, to make her stop her kidding, to be left alone, to get her out of my space, and here she fell, and next I knew she couldn't breathe, she was dead! I called the police, and ever since all hell broke loose on me."

All the sense of tragedy with which I'd lived these last months had evaporated. I was now hearing one of these banal stories that in one way or another millions of people experience throughout the world: a situation where a probably honest and helpless person gets caught in an unsolicited and dreadful adventure.

"Why do you want me to have killed a person, a woman," continued Fancy Lee, "disgusted, yes, I was disgusted, for one reason or another that's common in my job, but the world would be a cemetery if we responded that way every time we couldn't stomach something like that. And for me to be stuck here, isn't that disgusting too? I'm telling you, it was an accident, I say it over and over and they keep wanting to put my life on the line. It's cruel. It's unfair. Who's going to get me out of this shit. Nobody. Nobody. They're all busy fucking. I have never been bad. I'm a good person. As a matter of fact, though I try not to overdo it, I like taking taxi cabs. I love the yellow-colored ones, particularly. In the spring I see them as beautiful yellow flowers floating down the avenues."

Part Two

Listen, Hassan...

This boiling sun is driving me crazy. I miss California. I came to this country to get rid of counterfeit dollars. Are you listening? To exchange rotten dollars for good ones. As if money could be good! Back home, large posters enjoin us to "keep California green" and people laugh. They certainly would like their hills to be covered with green bucks. Yes, Hassan, I came to blanket Syria with fake money. I miss California, Hassan: its smell of gasoline, the vibrancy of its small towns and those highways on which I was rolling, a girl next to me, each day a new girl. I was a man, at fourteen, Hassan, and now... women are dead for me.

The dreadful sun of Damascus hammers its nails into my head. The police haunt me because they're so disgusting. Back home, our policemen are fast, they move on violent motorcycles. They are athletes. They have flair and speed and drink a plenty.

Today, I would have liked California to be flesh, a being on whom I could rest my hands. Would have liked her to be in this room. She smells of garages, of unwashed dogs, I know all that, but she gave me a childhood of happiness.

One has no friends in my country, Hassan, one has buddies. You can speak to whoever you want. In this city, in Damascus, I turn in circles and end up alone in my bed. No one to share my sweat with, no one to glue my skin on. I hate washing myself, Hassan, with each shower I take I feel a little bit more naked, a little bit more lonely.

We've already gotten rid of one suitcase, a big beast of a suitcase with millions in its belly. Money is dirty enough, and when it's fake it's sheer poison. In this oldest of cities, I, coming from a young country, have injected a syringe of death. I just received another shipment. And then I shall be free. I will never have to work again.

This boiling sun is exasperating. It brings out in me a hatred with no receiving end. I need to hate, Hassan. I spend hours, days, nights, pacing the floor like a beast in a cage. When you are not around to translate the Arabic newspapers for me, I am left with nothing to do. As soon as the new bills are on the market I'll get out. No Arab countries anymore. I am through with them. No Asia either, no Africa, I want to go home, buy one of these cars that I can wash everyday… maybe find myself a wife… some impudent and frigid woman who will chew at my identity.

I love you, Hassan, because you are silent. Back home everybody keeps talking. Everybody has something to say about the weather. You, you can keep your mouth shut. You made me love silence. You let me talk to you, you swim in my words and do not desert me. The day you washed your hands carefully and silently after manipulating my dollars for the first time I understood that I had found a real friend.

Damascus taught me what love in its immediacy could be. I had no previous ties, no memories attached to it. What I loved were the narrow streets that smelled of cheese, the markets that smelled of camel's urine, fountains that smelled of mud. Here I discovered the desire to become a bird, a dog, a donkey. I saw with my own eyes the narrow thread that separates us from the animal world, if a thread there is! One hardly encounters animals in my country. They are already dead and cut up and sterilized when you meet them…

When I stayed here day after day without any love-making something in me got attached to the city, the city that now satisfies the obscure itch which inhabits my limbs and my eyes. The people of Damascus hide their women, while it's their city I'm after. I brought to them bills loaded with crime and their cupidity has absorbed them. In exchange they gave me the centuries inscribed in the very dust I breathe.

God! Did I suffer in this city when I arrived! The flies on the hanging meat, the children with sick eyes, the beggars. I told myself it wasn't people I was dealing with but a race of lice. Back home everything is so clean, so clinical.

listen, hassan…

I met you, Hassan, in the marketplace when you came to offer your services, and I decided immediately that you would be the translator of my will. In your sad eyes I saw that you needed money. You always seem to be longing for something, desperately. I lied to you when I pretended I had lost the way to my room. I wanted you to serve my plans and in return I was going to serve your need to acquire objects. Since then, you are my interpreter, you stand between the jails of your country and my suitcase. When I have poured the last phony bills on the market I'll give you genuine money, money with which you're going to buy the things you want with no fear of being caught.

The first thing I noticed in Damascus, Hassan, was the sun. Its light has a golden hue I ignored. It has a quality I can't describe. It mesmerizes me. In California, we love the sky. The children buy astronomy books. Not having much of a past, I suppose we are trying to conquer a space more gigantic than anything the imagination has fathomed. We love stars, Hassan, even if we've lost the habit of looking at them. I had always thought that the sun was American.

I discovered here a yellow sun foreign to California's. I even had the madness, discovering it, to think that I was going to settle in Damascus forever. The idea lasted for a while. Little by little, like a virus, the sun had entered my mind and replaced me in my own brain. Now, Hassan, I have an enemy. I don't know yet whom I love or will love, but I know what I must absolutely avoid. I'm running away from the sun.

Today I'm particularly sick. I need one of these California Octobers, one of these slow evenings that follow the euphoria of winning a football game. Those nights, our girls with their perfect teeth, those nights in the cars, they're flexible… The prestige of a ride next to a boy haunts them like a vulture. In Damascus I see no victory that I can share. I see no victory at all.

Why do they keep telling me that we're a young nation? We're not any younger than the world itself. I know that when driving on the California highways, I often stared at some kind of a big hole in front of me. I was about twenty when I started seeing that black hole. Maybe that's why I left.

Put on the radio, Hassan. No, not the prayers again. Find me a station with some jazz, and get out. I'll see you tomorrow.

Hassan, I searched for you frantically. I went to your home and your parents slammed the door in my face. They didn't use to do that. Your little brother followed me, sticking out his tongue. I reached toward him and he ran away, screaming.

Something horrible happened. Sunday, I went out, just to do something. I walked by the river. It had so little water, a sewer more than a river! I went down to the souk and by the mosque and a bit further.

Hassan, what do women do when they're not married? Where do they go? They seem to be always together, looking at each other, giggling. What do they do with so much silence around them? They seem to look at everybody and everything with contempt. It's maddening.

Sunday, in the afternoon, it was hot and when the weather is that way, I start dreaming of girls. A habit. I don't like to be alone when the temperature rises. I can lose my mind. That's when the body of a woman can be a pool, a way out of my misery. And the sun was burning. My enemy was having a triumph in the sky.

Put on the radio. Find me some jazz! A drop of water in this desert. They tell you that jazz is cool but I say it's sheer alcohol. Frozen at first, it burns in your veins in a matter of seconds. And all these minarets spitting words I will never understand. I know guys back home who would sneer at these towers, with their pre-recorded prayers!

Hassan, I don't know how you'll take what I'm going to tell. It was horrible. I will never be able to touch a woman innocently. I will have to wash and wash myself. I have to unload this stone pressing on my heart. I found a small house, a little square of a room on the roof of a store, at the end of Suk el-Hamidiyeh, by the right side of the mosque. They told me that I could go ahead, that her own brother was her manager.

This city is going to get me. When I entered that

big hole, that darkish room, excuse me if I had to fuck, but what did I find, I found, still sitting on her chair and collapsed over herself, the prostitute that I had come for, murdered. I learned later that it was her brother who had done the killing. He'd discovered that all the money she was bringing in lately was fake, non-negotiable. In his anger he smashed her. Hassan, those are our rotten bills, we are the killers... and we still have stacks of them.

I looked for you all over the city. I was terrified, alone with my terror. I needed to talk with you, to see you. I wanted you to buy me some liquor, to watch over me...

Are you hearing the radio? That's Ellington's band. I was a teenager when Ellington wrote this melody. As I already told you, I was on my own then. A courageous little guy, imaginative. Camping alone. Had a small gun in the attic that I got from an older little fellow in exchange for my bicycle. I was whistling the blues. There was a bar with a jukebox but I was too young to be let in. So I used to sit on the sidewalk near the door, waiting for people to go in or out so that the music moved out with them, into the street, and I would catch some bits. Now they've built a garage at that corner.

Hassan, how can you not hate me? You're not uttering the slightest sound. I'm not really sorry for the dead woman, I can't explain how I feel, I'm numb. But from now on one thing is sure, there will be blood and horror on the face of every woman I try to approach. Not that I care much for them, Hassan, oh, I don't know a thing anymore, I suppose there isn't any happiness left for me in them. How would I ever make love to a nightmare?

I wish we were through with this money. Destroy it? I can't do that, the guys who sent me here will accuse me of having stolen it and will seek revenge on me in no time.

You see, when I made a deal with this gang I thought that I would leave them as soon as I was rich enough to call it quits. Real or fake, money is always just a piece of paper. For us Americans, it replaces many things. It's opium, Hassan, a drug the police don't mind.

At the door of my high school I remember there was a Mexican guy selling marijuana to us kids. I never gave in to the temptation and he resented it. But then, when I got this job, here in Damascus, in many of my dreams, I saw the Mexican staring at me, with some sort of a vindication, a vindication for so many things…

You're not answering. You're like all the Arabs: they seem to have expressive eyes but there's nothing in them I can read. It may be that they express only our own illusions. Maybe you're a people contemplating nothingness.

You're a people of imbeciles importing from my country the worst we can sell. Our obsolete machines. Smoke. Our dead objects. I was secretly hoping to find here some salt for my life. It's quite possible that I came for something other than money.

I love your face, Hassan. Your eyes brown and sad. The desperation they exude. The eyes I most remember from back home are those of dogs I encountered here and there. The most human things I saw in America, I think, were the faces of dogs. Do not mind, Hassan, I'm not trying to insult anyone. I love California because I've probably lost it. It's not my fault if I'm touched by dogs.

These Arabian songs that never stop are like my mind, which keeps throbbing. They remind me of our jazz music. But jazz is different. It brings me peace, whereas your songs make me want to scream.

You see, back home, a man enters a bar, watches a ballgame and you hear him pour his life's story to the guy sitting on the next stool. At this point, I have only you, you who I corrupted to the bone, and that doesn't make you stop looking at me with grateful eyes!

Since I saw this woman, this butchery, I have one thing in mind, to go away. I'll give you all that's left of the bills. You'll manage for both of us. I used to think that Ellington would get me out of anything, of any mood, but his music, tonight, I won't hear it. Those tunes, how to say it clearly, the purple hues they carry, their luxury, I think that Damascus has eliminated them for me forever.

Hassan, listen to me, you don't know Ellington, how could you? He's a man. He can turn noise into velvet. When I was young I was ready to die for him. He creates an ecstasy no woman has ever provided for me. There's more luxury in his music than in all the Cadillacs of Fifth Avenue. There's the whole of night in his orchestra and all the women one has never had.

Damascus has that bastard of a sun that beat me. Its smell of camels. Its smell of gazelles. I have not held many of its women in my hands. For me it's a city that has dried up. At first, I fell for its lines of bare hanging lightbulbs. Its leather market. Its defiant adolescents. Damascus must have survived through the power of its contempt. But contempt? I already have too much of it against myself.

Hassan, take this suitcase sitting over there, do something with it. I'll give you a better percentage this time. Now I must go out to dinner with the guy from my Consulate. He should go on suspecting nothing. I'll see you tomorrow.

ﻉﺲﻥ

This exploding sun, Hassan, I wish you'd take it away. The yellowish light that it casts on every wall will one day soften my brain. I wonder how you can walk while keeping your eyes open in this cruel light.

A few hours ago I sent them a telegram informing them that the deal went well. Who knows who our new victims are going to be? Whenever I touch money I try to imagine the lives of those who previously manipulated it. I'm going to be home soon. I'm a rich man. I'm rich even if you'd think that I'm not quite a man. You're also rich Hassan, and you're still looking sad. Your face did not change. It did change, yes, a bit, for anyone who knows you as well as I do. You see, if I had to do it again, if I were to meet you with the face you have today, I don't think I would bring you back with me to my hotel room. But you're the closest thing to what I would call a friend.

Now that all the money is poured on the market, I feel naked, relieved, but not any happier. I am going back to my small California hometown, to its sky of steel, its right angles. I'll buy me a wife and neighbors. Our streets are not as hypocritical as those in Damascus, one always knows where they lead to.

And you, Hassan, you will remain here. For a few more years, you'll play with your little brother and he'll wear the same pajamas. You won't tell them at home that you're rich. You'll start mentioning some unreal business and little by little show them your new power. Your sisters will listen to you. Your mother will bless you. She'll say that God has chosen you.

I wonder what I'll do when I go back. The months I've spent here have made me lose my footing. Our soldiers, on their return from Japan and Korea, started to miss those countries, while also hating them. They claimed that America looked empty. But I had never thought that there could be anywhere something we did not have already.

We have no mosques in our cities, but all kinds of churches, and monuments I never cared for. Our streets are never too messy and as for the slums, one never goes near them. There's nothing to do. I do remember, though, long afternoons of boredom, but even in the smallest towns one can find a place to go and have a drink.

In my telegram I also informed them that I was through with this job. "I did my part," I wrote, "and this kind of work doesn't interest me anymore." Tonight let's celebrate the fact that we are rich and free. We can afford to be extravagant, for example buy anything that attracts our fancy and throw it into the river. Hassan, today is feast day.

I will soon be gone from here. Let no one mention Arab countries to me again. It has been a strange experience that I want to forget. But I'm going to miss you. Where would I ever find somebody with those wounded eyes that you have? And somebody who lets me talk, who listens with the patience you're capable of. I'm turning my back to your country. I am through with it. Through!

It is the beginning of the afternoon. If it weren't so hot we would have gone out right now. But look, my enemy in the sky seems to quiver like a reflection in the river. The hour is so strange. I'm going out, Hassan, I'm going out to surrender myself to the police, the police I so despise…

Amal Hayati

It was midnight and through the branches the new moon was shining like Salaheddin's scimitar in a sky as pale and translucent as ancient Syrian glass… But with this moon rose a smell, unpleasant and disturbing.

My neighbor the grocer came to ask me if there was a dead rat somewhere. We looked together all over the house. It's true that the bathroom was not impeccable, that some water was leaking… but that was all.

Abu Ahmad left, then came back looking worried. The new moon as far as I know never affects the smells of the city. But yes, the breeze was warm.

For the last two weeks he has returned every morning. Yesterday he even brought along his helper and a little child who had just followed them.

He was right, the city was starting to stink…

Ahmad, his son, also came to visit me. He's a sergeant in the army, he rang and made his way in.

"Could you please," he said, "help me quiet my father down. He's obsessed with this question of garbage. Our government has too much to do to bother with this problem. You can't expect the Syrian Army to pick up run-over cats and rotten oranges."

"On my way back from the Djebel El Druze," I said, "the road was littered with dead donkeys covered with swarms of flies... where was the army?"

My remark seemed to upset him so much that I wondered if I shouldn't leave Damascus immediately, the young military dreading donkeys, the more when they're dead and filling the roads.

"Ahmad," I said, "your father is right. For years people have been throwing garbage every night on the sidewalks... It's such a mess."

Abu Ahmad appeared, a big smile on his face. He was obviously proud of his son's uniform. He spoke to him gently: "Ahmad, you're young and you're in the army and you can do something. You know that we're Muslims, and for us cleanliness is next to godliness. The enemy is at the door and our army is mobilized. It's up to the city to take care of such matters, but they're broke. All the money goes to the defense of the country. That's a sacred duty.

"Ahmad, you're my son and you're in the army... you can tell them that we can't sleep with this stench all around us. The people will die soon. This rottenness will get them."

Ahmad answered that there were secret and urgent missions to attend to and that the streets would be taken care of when the revolution completely succeeded. And that's when his father went into such a blind rage that I thought that his head was going to explode like a pomegranate. The old man started to shout:

"For twenty years now, the army has done nothing but feed its belly at our expense, we gave it our money, our work, our prayers, and all we have seen until now is dead Arabs; the enemy kills Arabs and the Arabs kill only other Arabs. Ahmad, I am tired. I want to die amid the scent of flowers, not of sewers."

Ahmad left.

സ്ക

The father was disappointed. Embarrassed. Worried for his city. Unhappy to see something he loved all his life deteriorate: the river in summer a garbage dump; the marketplace in the evenings a dumping ground; streets in the morning covered with garbage… He came to suspect that the minds were themselves littered with unhealthy thoughts.

I offered him something to eat, not wanting him to leave feeling humiliated. He accepted. I noticed that his sadness had gotten him down, that it wouldn't go away easily. I put on my record player, the first tape I found was Um Kulthum's. Fate decided that it be "Amal Hayati" and that song drilled deep into his soul. I don't know what ocean of sorrow brought down his inner barriers, but I saw a man age before my eyes and retire into an unreachable realm.

"Love me," Um Kulthum was pleading, and he was listening. Instead of losing the power of his passions, could the old man have transferred them, as through a prism, onto the city he had known all his life? The riots of 1936, the succession of Ramadans, the tanks of the French Army, the crates of apricots coming from the villages in the summers… "Love me," Um Kulthum was singing, "even if you have to curse me." But the curse was here, in the stench that the housewives were spreading on the sidewalks, the refuse that the trucks, which once in a while hauled the garbage, were leaving in their wake. This is how some sidewalks became permanently marked with malevolent traces, indelible signs.

The boy from the grocery store came to fetch Abu Ahmad. The latter was weary, preoccupied, having no desire to move on. He started telling me how his uncle, in his days, had been meticulous about cleanliness.

He evoked the courtyard's fountain, the rugs carefully stored at the first signs of summer, and the way, so precious, so annoying, that my own uncle had of crossing the smallest rivulet of water; you would have thought that he was on stilts, behaving like an ominous bird for whom any contact would be a blemish. "Your uncle," said Abu Ahmad, "was a good believer. He always made sure that his orchard was cleared of its dead leaves, he covered his property with pebbles and stones in order to keep down the dust, he spent hours choosing his meat." In my view, it wasn't so much an obsession with cleanliness as a chronic irritation with his environment, a discrepancy between him and his life.

Abu Ahmad did finally leave. But he stood a long time on the doorstep, considering all the consequences of the decision he was about to make: He would organize a neighborhood to demand from the government more efficient cleaning of the city's public spaces. I agreed. I was disgusted with the sight, all over the city, of these viscous, foul-smelling bags, lining the streets as if they were heaps of defused, old, and rotten grenades left behind by some disheartened troublemakers… the very image of a whole people's impotence.

"My love of yesterday," Um Kulthum was singing, "my love of today, my love of tomorrow…," a blanket of velvet over a city's stagnation.

Abu Ahmad, me, and the boy, for a few days we went from door to door, asking the people's support for a petition. We went gently, pushed no one, didn't insist… people seemed so used to the stench that they didn't even notice it, or pretended not to. The young were the worst: they would speak either of war or of the blue jeans they intended to buy; I can still see before me the face of that high-school student, the hardest I have ever seen, telling me: "Come on! We're the ones who stink, us the walking dead.

The whole city is just bad breath." Abu Ahmad thought that he was exaggerating, that things weren't that hopeless… He couldn't understand how anyone would accept living among so much dirt or how such a young person would be so bitter.

We managed to gather some fifteen people and the youngster joined us, as cynical as he was. The argument that won them over was the one dearest to Abu Ahmad's heart: that the lack of cleanliness was a sort of sacrilege painful to the Prophet's soul. Infections, epidemics, don't cause much alarm because when they progress like lightning they appear to be supernatural events proceeding from a divine decision. Our little procession got off, chanting *Allahu Akbar* and finally arrived at the door of the ministry where Ahmad was stationed.

A crisis was brewing. The news spread like fire, among the middle class, in the marketplaces, at the city gates, as far as the camel drivers' quarters; they were already talking, I learned later, of a bloody "counter-revolution."

Abu Ahmad asked to see his son. He was sure that his uniformed child had great powers. Ahmad was indeed a member of the security guard of the ministry, standing idly all day long. He felt both furious and worried when he saw that his father had come with his group of angry citizens. He stood there, as if he had never met the old man, as if he were facing a menacing object that had to be removed from his sight.

Abu Ahmad kept smiling proudly. He stepped ahead and tried to pull Ahmad toward him in order to whisper something in his ear. Then we saw him stop suddenly and stare at his hands as if, having touched the buttons of the uniform, they had gotten cold and scared.

A few soldiers inquired what it was all about. We saw them split their sides with laughter at the idea that we were concerned with garbage. They shouted in unison:

"We're the backbone of the country, we're busy with serious matters. Out of here!"

"That's why we came," pleaded Abu Ahmad, "Please call your commander, we have a request. The civilians are good-for-nothings. But the army, that's something else. It can act quickly, it has all the power."

For a moment Ahmad was disarmed by what he considered to be his father's naiveté. He tried to appeal to his common sense, telling him: "Listen, the revolution will answer all our needs, give it time!"

The old man lost his temper: "What is this revolution that stinks! Yes, I swear to God that it stinks!"

Ahmad panicked. While he was trying to get into the compound soldiers were pouring out from every corner, were positioning themselves on the stairs and the street, and Abu Ahmad was standing all alone in the midst of chaos, ranting about the earlier years, that famous strike against the French occupation, the one that had paralyzed Damascus for almost two months… he was even throwing the Ottomans into the confusion.

Ahmad reappeared, flanked by two military policemen. His eyes were shining as much as his stripes. He was shouting: "Go away, go away, stop this madness, I have orders to stop this rioting, I will shoot!" He made it obvious that he meant what he said.

We all pulled back. Abu Ahmad was begging, "Please, please…," and I believe that he was still thinking of taking his son into his arms, of convincing him, of integrating him into his honor. But Ahmad shot at the crowd, and the old man collapsed on the threshold of the building.

Dead. Only the child from the grocery store moved toward him. Then he came back to me and with the seriousness of a child, he asked: "How can it be that Abu Ahmad is still crying after his death?" I explained to him that sometimes tears accumulated in the eyes run on their own, even after someone has died.

Abu Ahmad got a clean shroud for his burial at least. The group of people that accompanied him to the cemetery was the same one that had gone with him to the ministry. His son Ahmad led the cortège. I will never figure out if the grimace he had on his face was due to a feeling of deep sorrow or the pride of having done one's duty… after all he had the kind of attachment to the army that one usually feels for one's family.

We returned to our dark apartments. We cleaned neither our souls nor our streets.

"I accepted the world, I accepted love," sings Um Kulthum. We shall listen and listen, we shall drown in her voice, fade into it, oh yes, and she will die, and we will feel terribly lonely.

The Radio

The radio is broken; the son, dead; the father, insane. That's not some news read in the newspaper, it's what Omar is telling me.

"Omar, come here. How old are you?"

"Eleven, twelve…"

"Why are you crying?"

"I'm not crying."

"Yes, you are."

"I'm not crying. I'm selling safety pins."

"Since when are you selling safety pins, and where are they?"

"Since this morning, Madam."

"Are you crying because you're hungry?"

"I'm not hungry and I never cry."

"What's your name?"

"Omar, Omar ibn Abu Taleb. Monday, the neighbors' cat died. Tuesday, my father threw the radio and broke it. Taleb left the house. Wednesday, we waited all day for Taleb to return. Thursday, they declared that Father was insane. Saturday, they came and took him away. I'm here and I'm not crying. The city is over there and it's endless. God is great."

"Where do you live, exactly?"

"We live neither in a house nor out in the desert, but in a camp. There are no tents or hard walls to give us shelter but something in between that gives people the illusion of being housed. We're not cave dwellers, at least. Do we belong to the world? We're from nowhere and no century. None of the signs that make one part of the world are allowed to us: no passports, no professions, no government, no voting, no speaking. Like a table whose chair is in the next room, or a body whose severed head is in a suitcase or on a plane, our country is Palestine and we are in the south of Beirut, neither in the city nor outside it, always in some intermediary territory, as if in the midst of a dying forest. We have a view of the sea but we cannot go to it. It's permanently a mile and a half away. It's not that we don't know how to swim. Some of us have even learned to swim on our mattresses. Others have parents who knew how to swim very well even when the sea was restless. Yes, there, in front of us, there's a meeting of sea and sun that is the beginning of the world. But when it comes to us, we're not yet born. I live here and nobody ever buys anything."

"And why would you try to sell safety pins?

"To do like the kids who work in Hamra, where there are stores and jobs. Over here, there's only God. Here, there's the dream, and the radio. News from everywhere. Like in the big prisons. Men in prison are well informed. They have powerful radios. The world is an ocean of words. When the astronauts landed on the moon, they knew it in San Quentin, they knew it in Siberia, in Sabra and Shatila, they knew it in Hamra, in Paris at the Café de Flore, in Beijing… everywhere. Over radio stations, they announced everything except the sorrow."

"And your father, what does he do?"

"He was always sitting and listening to the news. In the morning, at seven, it's always the BBC. Their Arabic is good. Father thinks it's the best Arabic on the waves. Then he listened to Cairo. For music he always preferred Radio Lebanon. At night, he was glued to Radio Palestine. All the shelling and the dying are on that radio. Then we had the midday news. He was anxious to know if something important had happened since the morning, and then back to the BBC. When what he heard was too unpleasant, he would switch to Radio-Amman, or Voice of Syria. Sometimes he was inadvertently running into Radio Israel and he was hurriedly changing stations. For my mother, it's different. She cares for music and she listens to what she likes most, regardless. But I heard her say: 'They have even stolen Um Kulthum from us… but what the hell if her voice should come from Jerusalem!… it's still home, isn't it?! Um Kulthum sings in Jerusalem!'"

"Where was your father from?"

"From Haifa, Palestine. They owned a big garden,

over there, bigger than three or four houses put
together, and a house. All my uncles knew how to
swim because that city is a harbor and in those times
they could go anywhere they wanted. Here, you
must know how things are. Father told us again and
again that he was five years old when the family had
to leave. They were scared. Scared of the English.
Scared of the Jews. Scared of the radios. Scared of
graffiti on the walls. At the end, I believe, scared of
themselves. They went first to Jericho. We still have
family there. My father worked like a laborer on the
fields although he had owned a store with one of my
uncles. He worked hard; the land was dry, the rains
scarce, the sun blinding. A few days ago, he was still
mentioning the sand storms of Jericho. And then, in
1967, Gamal Abdel Nasser lost the war. His radio
was saying one thing, Damascus's another. The
enemy had also his own story to tell. After June 7,
1967, Father never put on their station. He even
used to curse it. That's what Mother said. A new exo-
dus started for them. They ended up in Lebanon
with only their clothes on, and Father's black little
radio. Taleb, my brother, was barely four years old, I
was told. I came after. If you can call this place a
home, then it's my home."

"What about your mother?"

"My mother's name is Khadijah. She's very beautiful but she always fights with Father. Always. The
neighbors will come and stop them."

"How did Taleb die?"

"I'll tell you. It was not too long ago, on a day when everything went wrong. My mother was in a terrible mood because the neighbors had come to tell her that Taleb had killed their cat just like that, out of viciousness. That wasn't true at all. Father was following Sadat's speech on the radio and my mother tried to get his attention and they were both very upset, and I remember her shouting at him that he was losing his time, that Sadat had been mean to Um Kulthum, out of jealousy, of course. She went on and on repeating that in her opinion President Sadat was a good-for-nothing, a man caring only for his Suez Canal and the big boats that were crossing it. He should have been an admiral! Father got impatient with her, with us, his voice was rising, he was shouting that the Suez Canal had not been built for the Egyptian fleet but for the oil of the Arabs.

"Taleb joined the fray. He was livid with anger. He told them to shut up and that was close to sacrilege. He blamed the 'evil box' for the fact that he was ignorant, that he hadn't ever learned to read and write, because of the noise filling the single room we occupied and all the foreign voices that were entering our space like as many monsters tormenting our minds.

"Father was livid with anger. He answered that since his birth all he ever did was wait, wait, but not for a Messiah nor for the Last Judgment. All of us are like our ancestor Job, he insisted, that man from the desert, from the other side of the Jordan River, and fate had decided that he would be our model, an incitement for the Arabs to be as patient as he was. There are tens of thousands of people like us, here, in this camp, in Kuwait, in Africa, Canada, America... listening and waiting. Everywhere there's a normal life with food, work, sleep, but when it comes to us, we have oversize ears and we listen. We zip from one radio station to another: those are our travels.

"'When are you going to stop it,' said my mother vociferously, 'you drive us crazy with this object! I raised the kids, year after year washed office floors at UNWRA's headquarters, and what did you do? I know what you did, with this satanic object you introduced into this room, day and night, unbearable noises made by maddened birds that are making me lose my mind. I pray God to curse you all!'

"I think that Father, at that moment, believed that God was going to break his radio. He started to shout, 'the neighbors throw stones at my son, my wife complains ad infinitum, and God wants to immure me! I myself will shatter this radio into pieces, silence these words, these rivers of words. Facing me is this mountain staring at me and Time, that God created, is falling into dust. It's me who will destroy everything, it's not God who will do it, nor my wife, it's me, me!' He threw the radio through the open door and it went dead. We were stupefied. A heavy silence fell upon us, taking possession of us and clogging our eyes, ears, and throats."

"Did your father lose his mind right then?"

"I don't know. But immediately after, Taleb announced to us that he resolved to go to Palestine however he could and whatever the price. He left. My mother went to search for him, in the camps, at the different Palestinian organizations, in the streets. Nobody had the slightest clue. That's what they told her. And then, on Thursday evening, she came back from the neighbors, screaming, 'Taleb is dead! Voice of Palestine said that Taleb has died, that Taleb is dead!' Taleb died while crossing the border with a group of fedayeens. They didn't want to take him along, at first, he was too young and lacked training. Taleb died in Lebanon but I'm sure his blood trickled into Palestine. Taleb never lied. If he said that he would go there it means he did, dead or alive.

"I could say that father aged instantly. He looked as if he were the oldest man in the camp, his face twitching, his legs shaking. He started to mumble uninterruptedly, 'The BBC killed Taleb. The BBC killed Taleb…' Then he became incoherent, 'Taleb is swimming in the Dead Sea, Taleb is swimming in the Jordan River. Taleb is swimming in Lake Tiberias. He is swimming under the Occupied Territories like the god of the Pharaohs…' He seized an ax and split the chair in two, he hacked out the door and the bed. He threatened my mother with his weapon, he howled like a wolf. The neighbors came running. They called the police that are in charge of the camp. They took him to the hospital, the type of hospital where they keep people for a long time. That's what they said. All this happened last week. It burns in my head. My mother told me: 'You're the only man left to me. I have no one but you.' So, you see, I'm a man, now. I sell safety pins. I don't cry. She's the one who cries in her room."

"Where are you going to sell them? Who's going to buy?"

"Nobody. There aren't any businesses around. Everything happens in the city: banks, stores, places to eat out… in this camp, the only foreigners who come are journalists or spies. These people are stingy. They bring nothing to us but words. That's when they don't bring trouble. Are you a journalist? I wouldn't think you are."

"No. I'm not a journalist. What are you going to do?"

"You don't have to worry. Nothing happens here but what you see: some people live, some die. They wait. What for? Nobody cares. These safety pins, they're not eatable. I will try for a while and then God only knows what I'll do. Taleb is dead. My parents are alive, but what can I say. Palestine is alive. It is there, south of Southern Lebanon. Where many people die. Many. There's not any fall season because there aren't any trees. It's our men who fall like autumn leaves. Not all of them. Some go and return. They say: 'Palestine smells good. She's worth our lives.' But I'm not going to die. How can I? I'm not yet born. I will be born over there, on the road to Haifa, as in the days of my grandparents."

A Stream Near Damascus

The light, in that late afternoon, was showing itself under the colors of gray and yellow, and the birch trees were screening it here and there like a strainer. The soil was screaming for water. Unable to bear for long the ordeal of a Damascus heat, my sister-in-law and I went to a nearby village where we knew a clearing by the side of a stream. It was one of those streams, no larger than some four feet, that lazily cross the valley of the Barada River and irrigate the orchards of Arab poetry or, more prosaically, wash the feet of the peasants or are used by them for drinking. The children bathe in them naked while their mothers get close carefully, wearing their white scarves on their heads.

There's always an exquisite freshness, sweet to the spirit as well as to the skin, brutalized by the rigor of the Syrian summer. We went to sit by the cemented edge of the stream, our legs dangling in the cool water. At the level of our knees there was a line dividing the world in two: underneath there was limpidity and coolness and above dryness and heat. This is how the two worlds that rule the valley are juxtaposed, as if the waterways of this country were not penetrating the earth but rather sliding like mercury on arid grounds that refuse to absorb them. In the Syrian villages one can repeat, after the poet, that the soul dies of thirst next to a fountain.

A diaphanous shape, dressed in white, came toward us, a woman. She smiled to us, and, looking at the current, talking to herself in a dream-like voice, she said: "Don't think that this is a small stream, one can die in it. The other day, a fifteen-year-old girl, daughter of Kuwaitis who come every spring for their vacation, fell, and the current carried her away. She must have not known how to swim. When they found her, her body was bruised and swollen, her eyes were immobile and open. Her belly was enormous. The water had raped her. A young man came to the rescue. He entered the river and swam faster than the current as the body was floating far out along the bank and he grabbed it and laid it on the ground. We believed that she was dead. But he must possess forbidden powers, and God bless our Prophet, the young man seemed to whisper in her ear and he breathed into her mouth, they were mouth to mouth like strange lovers, and, God protect us, he resurrected her! O God, save the world from all evils!"

Thus we were, the three of us sitting silently when we saw, floating, descending, a tree trunk with two branches spread like human arms, immersed in the water. The scene made me quiver; it was like a recollection.

All of a sudden, my companion, the peasant woman, rose and tried to grab the trunk by one of its branches. I seized the other. The stream was accelerating. The woman was saying that she had to save that big piece of wood, which could be dried out and used for fire. The speed of the current proved to be too much for us.

Some men came by: one, two, three of them, pulling together to no avail. A shadow moved through the birch trees and the peasant woman sent a shriek in its direction. A young man wearing baggy pants walked toward us, looked fixedly at the waters and, pushing aside one of the men, pulled out the injured and wet trunk and deposited it tenderly on a dusty soil eager to drink some unexpected water. He placed the object the way one abandons a beloved body, and as if participating in some strange ritual he walked away and disappeared.

The men tried to follow him. This piece of wood was of no interest to them anymore. They gave it to us, the women. The peasant woman refused to have anything to do with it. My sister-in-law found it most cumbersome, and I had no need for it, being just on a visit. The peasant spit noisily; it was a traditional way to chase away evil spirits. Then, turning around, she shook her head and told us: "You have seen this young man already, haven't you? That was him, the savior!"

That evening I went with my brother to one of the cafés that border the western entrance to Damascus. He named for me what he called "the seven rivers" that run on parallel lines along the little resort town of Dummar, and are in fact extremely modest but with a charm of their own. The Barada, at the bottom of its narrow valley, was flowing rapidly. From everywhere in the dark and under the electric bulbs suspended from tree to tree, there was water, running and fresh, one of the streams being the one on whose bank I was sitting not too many hours ago. We were drunk with the pleasure of being near so much water in a warm wind that was reminding us of the proximity of the desert. The night was scintillating with stars: it looked like a mixture of black metal and distant light. I was thinking of its incredible beauty when I saw, sliding on the lowest of the streams, just where the latter was joining the river, a kind of a shadowy figure in baggy pants, embracing a tree trunk the way one holds in one's arms the body of the beloved. And I still hear my brother's voice telling me, as the creature was, with the moving water, entering a zone of darkness: "There goes the giver of life, holding her in his arms and walking on the waters!"